Lisa

SpringSong ❦ Books

Lisa

Betty Shaffer

BETHANY HOUSE PUBLISHERS
MINNEAPOLIS, MINNESOTA 55438

Lisa
Betty Shaffer

Library of Congress Catalog Card Number 82-72149

ISBN 1-55661-449-7
Betty Shaffer
Copyright © 1982

Published by Bethany House Publishers
A Ministry of Bethany Fellowship, Inc.
11300 Hampshire Avenue South
Minneapolis, Minnesota 55438

Printed in the United States of America

BETTY SHAFFER is married to Howard Shaffer, M.D., and the mother of three grown children. She was educated at Westminster College, and has taken a number of literature and writers' courses since graduation. She came to Christ as a child, found her faith severely tested during college years, married her husband the day after his graduation from medical school, and now resides in western Pennsylvania.

1

It was third period study hall when Lisa Carson first realized that Brandon Danforth was looking at her. He kept turning around, staring past the fellow in front of her, and smiling in her direction. She glanced over her shoulder to see who was behind her and then blushed when she realized she was in the last seat in the row.

Does he want to borrow my English homework? she wondered. He had never asked for her paper before. Other girls were usually eager to let him have theirs. She thought it was dishonest to copy homework, and most kids knew how she felt, but maybe today he was in a jam. Could she refuse him if he asked?

Her hands grew so sweaty that her pencil slipped through her fingers and dropped to the floor, rolling toward Brandon's seat. She got up and stooped to retrieve it. Brandon bent his head close to her and his fingers gently closed over her hand as they reached for the pencil at the same time. An electric current shot through her as he continued to hold her hand firmly. "I hear you and Todd Putnam were getting pretty friendly on the bus last weekend," he whispered close to her ear.

Lisa's cheeks felt hot as she pulled away from him.

How did Brandon know about Todd? Brandon wasn't on the bus.

"How about sitting with me at the basketball game tomorrow night?" he asked as she straightened up.

"What about the girl from Monroe High?" she shot back at him, covering her confusion with an angry tone and avoiding his eyes. Lisa knew he had gone steady for several months.

"She won't be coming to our game," Brandon said with a knowing smile.

The teacher had risen from her desk and was stalking toward the back of the room with her eyes on Lisa. She hurried back to her seat without answering Brandon. She needed to finish her algebra assignment. All her ninth-grade classes seemed to require more work than those of the first two years of junior high, but she couldn't concentrate on algebra now.

She sat staring out the window at the nut tree bareboned against the cold sky. A few empty pods still clung to the top branches, but Lisa didn't really see them. Brandon's question filled her thoughts. *Why did he ask me?* she wondered. Was it the kiss she let Todd give her on the bus after the Friday night game that made Brandon interested? She should never have let Todd kiss her, but it just sort of happened without either of them saying anything.

When they boarded the bus to come home, Debbie Freeman, whom she had gone with, wanted Lisa to change seats so Debbie could sit with Lane Raymond. Lisa had been upset with Debbie and at first hadn't said much to Todd. He wasn't in any of her classes, she hardly knew him, and besides, he was overweight and certainly not her type. But in the darkened bus, conversation became easy and she found herself telling Todd how her parents got things for her little sister, Jenny, that Lisa wouldn't have dared ask for. Todd was a good listener, and when he put a comforting arm around her shoulder, she didn't resist.

When Todd's face came close to her for a kiss, Lisa didn't draw back, though the whole thing seemed cold and mechanical. In the school parking lot as they got off the bus, he didn't say anything about seeing her again, and neither did she.

That Friday night for the first time she could remember, Lisa fell into bed without praying. God was far from her thoughts. She was young and wanted to live like everyone else.

When Lisa was ten she had said yes to Jesus Christ as her Savior at a special meeting in their church. She really meant it when she asked Jesus into her heart, but she had been too shy to go forward when the evangelist had given the altar call.

Lisa had tried to read her Bible through as the evangelist had suggested, but she had bogged down in Leviticus and counted the Bible portion her parents always read at breakfast with their devotional guide as her own Bible reading for the day. She had always prayed at bedtime, though she said much the same thing every night, and had never really seen prayer make much difference in spite of the stories she heard in church.

Lisa was fifteen and no one had ever asked her for

a date. Lots of girls in her class had been dating since seventh grade.

The boys at church sometimes called her "Stork" or "Stilts," making her feel lanky and unattractive. Her legs *were* long, and after studying them in the mirror, she decided they *were* stilts. Mother had said with a smile, "The boys are only trying to get your attention. In a few years things will be different."

Lisa didn't want to wait a few years. She wanted the boys to show they liked her now. She hated their teasing, and it was exciting to have a boy want to date her at last! Especially Brandon. Her heart beat faster. She couldn't believe it.

She had noticed Brandon the first day of junior high. She couldn't help it because he had called Miss Golan "Babe," and the pretty young teacher had laughed at him and had made some crack about "Lover Boy." Everyone had laughed, even Brandon, and the whole uptight class seemed to relax as if a bolt of lightning had discharged the electricity of fear in the air.

Self-assurance shone from his bright blue eyes, smiling engagingly from under the shock of reddish brown hair falling over his forehead. He was built like a football player, his shoulders broad from lifting weights. She knew this because she had heard him discussing weight lifting with Kevin Carpesino. She knew, too, he had been held back in grade school, was sixteen, and drove a cherry red Corvette.

In homeroom and study hall he sat two seats ahead of her, with Kevin in between. It seemed to her as if the air around Brandon was charged like a magnetic field, drawing her attention to him like a needle pointing north. He often turned around to talk to Kevin, and she could always overhear the conversation, but she didn't think he knew she existed. It was ridiculous, but sometimes she felt like pelting him with anything she could lay her hands on—pencils, erasers, even books. Of course she never did, never admitting to anyone how he affected her, not even Debbie, her closest friend at school. Debbie talked about boys all the time, and Mom said Debbie was boy crazy, but at least she didn't do drugs. Lisa didn't have much choice of friends in school since the kids from church lived in another district.

Debbie had liked Brandon for a while in the fall. She had tried, while Lisa stood by with burning cheeks, to get him to take her home after a football game. That was before he had started dating the girl from Monroe. He had ignored Debbie consistently, and later they saw him driving by with one of the senior high cheerleaders.

What would Debbie think if Brandon wasn't kidding when he asked Lisa to sit by him? More important, what would her parents think? Her mother said sixteen was soon enough to start dating, but maybe they wouldn't mind if she just sat with a boy at a basketball game. Lisa certainly wouldn't say anything to him unless he spoke to her again.

When the study-hall bell rang, Lisa edged herself around the back of the room and lost herself in the crowd pressing out the door. She didn't see Brandon until English class when he turned around and winked at her across the room. She smiled faintly, feeling the blood rising in her cheeks, and ducked her blond head over her grammar. She was angry with herself. Brandon really was showing some interest in her and she was dodging him. It didn't make sense, or did it?

The next day he was late for homeroom, and it was one of her health-class days, so she wasn't in study hall. Tonight was the game. She had persuaded her mother after school yesterday to let her buy the soft blue sweater she had been wanting to go with her new jeans. But she hadn't mentioned Brandon to her mother. Why should she? Brandon would probably ignore her today.

She managed to miss Brandon on the way into English class, but they hadn't been seated long when Brandon got up to go to the pencil sharpener. She was aware of his moving up her aisle, but she didn't look up. As he passed her desk he casually dropped a piece of folded paper on it.

When he was back in his seat, she opened the note. "Meet me outside the door after class" was all it said, and was signed with a swirling B characteristic of his left-handed writing. She often watched with fascination as he curled his hand around to write with a flourish in the same direction as right-handed people.

Seeing him standing in the hall waiting for her sent an electric current dancing through her tummy.

"Can I pick you up for the game?" he asked.

Lisa stood straight, but she still had to look up to meet his sparkling eyes. She looked directly into them and felt an answering light dancing in her own amber eyes.

"You'd better not come to the house. I don't think

my parents would like it," she said.

He shrugged. "Okay. I'll wait for you by the ticket window. You'll come for the preliminaries, won't you?"

She nodded and added, "I've got a season ticket. I can meet you inside." That way it wouldn't be a date, she rationalized.

"Okay, Babe. See you later," he said and dashed for the steps to gym class.

Lisa wished she could escape Debbie, who was conveniently lingering in the hall. She felt as though she had been bungee jumping and wanted time to enjoy the sensation. Debbie fell into step beside her.

"Hey, what was that all about?" she demanded. She'd have to tell Debbie because they always sat together even if Debbie had some guy in tow.

"Brandon wants me to sit with him tonight," she said.

"Wow!" Debbie exclaimed. "Not bad! But you better watch him. He's got quite a reputation, you know."

Lisa knew, but just then she didn't care. She just wanted to savor that marvelous sensation.

She'd think about his reputation later.

2

The nut tree was blooming with new spring life, the buds were swelling, but Lisa didn't see them as she sat staring out the study-hall window. She was aware of the algebra book unopened on her desk and fumbled with it. She had to do her homework or fail the day's assignment again. She couldn't afford to have that happen much more this six weeks. She forced herself to open the book, but all the little a's, b's, and x's ran together. She couldn't focus on them. Her attention was on the cold hand gripping her stomach.

My period didn't start this morning. Lisa didn't need to remind herself, but she did. She had willed it to come, and now she tried to convince herself that it was starting, but she was afraid it wasn't.

Maybe it's because I've been so upset lately. Once after I had a fight with my counselor at camp, I didn't have a period all summer. But she knew this was different.

She glanced at Brandon's seat in study hall. It was empty. Shot put was his sport, and he had talked his way out of study hall to practice for the upcoming track season. But she hardly saw him anymore anyway. She dropped her head on her arms, covering her algebra book. Behind her closed eyes Lisa's thoughts swirled.

Why, oh, why, had she ever let herself get involved with Brandon?

The first night he sat with her at the game had been great. Lisa walked with her shoulders back and her head high as Brandon went out with her after the second quarter of the senior high game. He offered to buy her a Coke.

"Don't you want one?" she asked as he handed her the paper cup.

"I've got something better in the car," he winked. "The real stuff. Come on out with me for a few minutes. We need some fresh air anyway."

Did a bell ring in the school, or was it a warning bell sounding inside her own head? She couldn't be sure, but she didn't want to listen. It felt good to have someone as popular as Brandon paying attention to her.

In the car he reached over the backseat and pulled up a can, popped the lid, and took a long swig. "Ah," he said, "that's better."

There wasn't enough light to read the label, "It's beer, isn't it?" she said.

"You betcha. Great stuff! Ever taste it?" he asked.

"No, I . . . we don't believe in drinking. That is, my parents don't."

"Why not?"

"They just don't believe Christians should drink." She hated the direction the conversation was taking. She didn't want to get into an argument with Brandon. She just wanted to have some fun.

"It doesn't say in the Bible you shouldn't drink," Brandon challenged. "I went to Sunday school for a while when I was a kid. I know something about the Bible."

She sipped her own drink and didn't answer. Involuntarily she shivered. Brandon noticed. "Hey, Babe, are you cold?" He slid close beside her and slipped his arm around her shoulder. "This stuff'll warm your innards," he coaxed. "How about a taste?"

Lisa was curious to know what it tasted like. Those TV ads really made it look good and innocent. Surely one little taste wouldn't hurt.

"Here, let me give you a preview." Brandon turned his head and blew his breath playfully into her face. "Better yet," he said and pressed his open lips against her supple mouth. A golden light flashed behind Lisa's closed eyes. A caution light? She returned the kiss.

As he pulled back from her, he took another swallow from the can he still held in his left hand. "Come on, try it." He tilted the can to her lips. She sputtered as the sour liquid hit her mouth.

"It's not sweet. It tastes like it's spoiled."

He laughed. "I'll tell you one thing that isn't spoiled. That kiss was sweet enough. How about another?" Lisa offered no resistance.

That night Lisa insisted they go back to the game, and her father picked her up as usual. At breakfast she casually mentioned to her mother that Brandon had sat with her, and her mother promptly began to question her about him. She wanted his whole history, and Lisa was glad she could at least tell her he had gone to Sunday school. Her mother finally conceded that it was probably okay for him to sit with Lisa, but reminded her that she wasn't allowed to date for another year.

The next game was away and Brandon wanted to drive her there, but her parents said "No!" She knew it was useless to argue.

"Your parents sure are old-fashioned," Brandon charged, and she had to agree.

He refused to go on the bus and didn't suggest sitting with Lisa. Instead, wearing his blue and white track jacket, he arrived at the game with the girl from Monroe and chose a seat below Lisa. She was sure he did it on purpose to punish her. With a sick feeling in her stomach, she missed most of the game because she was watching Brandon talking and laughing with the other girl.

The next time he asked her to ride with him, she didn't ask her parents. They met at the school, and he brought her back in time to meet her father, though they left the game at intermission and parked on the way back. There had been more beer and more passionate kisses. When Lisa worried that her father would smell the beer, Brandon produced a roll of mint candies.

The pattern was set. They left earlier from each game and kissing led to more. Lisa found she didn't want to—or couldn't—stop. She was never sure which.

As things got out of hand, Lisa began to feel guilty. She had learned the Ten Commandments in Vacation Bible School, including "Thou shalt not commit adultery," but when she tried to tell Brandon this, he argued convincingly that you couldn't commit adultery unless you were married. Then she told him she'd been taught sex is for marriage. But he only laughed at her old-fashioned idea. In the passion of the moment, he won. Why, she wondered, did she always give in to him? Could it have been the little bit of beer?

Little bit? Maybe a can! Brandon drank two or three and she kept taking a few sips at a time. It made her feel relaxed and confident. She decided not to drink any more beer. She wouldn't let it happen again.

But at the next game when she insisted they not leave early, Brandon walked away and left her sitting alone. Lisa felt cold, even in the overheated gym. She looked around for Debbie and saw her sitting with Lane on the top bleacher. She couldn't make a spectacle of herself by climbing up there.

Lisa hunched her shoulders over her knees and leaned her head on her hands. She couldn't go home. Her father wouldn't arrive for a couple of hours. Finally, she raised her head and looked for Brandon. He was by the open door laughing with the cheerleader he had taken home in the fall.

"Brandon, oh, Brandon! I want to go with you!" she cried inside. Like someone hypnotized, Lisa got up and followed him.

When he saw her coming, he broke away from the girl he was talking with and gave Lisa a big grin. "Ready to go, Babe?" He caught her elbow and propelled her through the door. Her pulse quickened. If only she could persuade him to settle for kissing!

She tried. She refused the beer. They argued, but somehow it lent spice to the occasion. "It's harmful for both of us not to be natural," he reasoned. "If it feels right, it is right." Brandon won again.

Lisa determined she wouldn't think about it anymore. What happened, happened. She couldn't help it. Still when she crawled into bed, even without praying, something nagged.

Then came the awful night when time got away from them completely. As they approached the high school, the parking lot was empty—except for one car. She knew whose it was.

Lisa was struggling to comb the snarls out of her long, thick hair and sucking frantically on her mint as they stopped as far from the other car as possible. A familiar square figure sprang from the parked car and strode toward them.

"Dad'll be furious. What'll we tell him?" Lisa appealed to Brandon.

"I don't know. I'm afraid that's your problem," Brandon said smoothly.

The comb caught and twisted in her hair. She couldn't get it loose. "I can't get the comb out of my hair!"

"Keep trying. It'll come."

The square figure was getting close. She jerked on the comb again, pulling her hair until she thought she would have a bald spot. Finally the comb broke and she disentangled the pieces just as Brandon reached across her and shoved the door open. "Good luck. You'll handle it okay."

For a split second Lisa was too stunned to move. *Is he really going to let me face Dad alone? But I'll have to sooner or later.* She sprang to life. "Thanks for nothing!" she said as she scrambled out of the car and slammed the door with all her might.

Lisa came face-to-face with her father, but the shadows veiled his expression. Still she well knew the set of his shoulders.

"Lisa Anne Carson, where have you been?" His voice was its sternest. The Corvette behind her took off with the engine roaring and tires screeching. Lisa ran her fingers over the jagged edges of the broken comb in her pocket.

"Is that Brandon?" her father demanded.

"Let's go home." Lisa's knees were shaking. "I guess it's kind of late."

"Late! I've been waiting for you at least an hour. Debbie said you'd gone off with Brandon! I thought we had that settled."

"Dad, I'm sorry. We just took a little ride." She tried to calm him and her own pounding heart.

"My daughter doesn't go riding around in cars at fifteen years of age or any other age unless I know where she's going and when she's coming back." His white, angry face stared at Lisa. He turned away. "But let's go. We'll settle this at home."

Of course Lisa wasn't allowed to go to any more basketball games. Her mother quizzed her about what she and Brandon were doing, but Lisa kept insisting they had only gone for a ride.

Lisa had been so furious with Brandon that she had avoided him ever since . . . or had he avoided her? She raised her head now and glanced at his empty seat in study hall.

What if my period doesn't start? What else can I do? Maybe I can use the trampoline in gym. She was afraid of it, but if she fell, it might bring it on.

What if I'm really pregnant? It was the first time she had dared ask herself that question. *Can I tell Brandon? Who else can I tell? Debbie? No, Debbie warned me about Brandon. How could I have been so stupid?* She remembered with wonder the warm currents he created in her, and feared he could again.

Getting pregnant, having a baby, hadn't been on her agenda, at least not for many years. Lisa was going to be a nurse. Her mother had had one year in nursing and dropped out to marry her father. They had gone together in high school, and when he went directly into his dad's plumbing business, he didn't want to wait for her to finish training to get married.

She guessed her mother hadn't regretted it, but she talked a lot about Lisa being a nurse, what good opportunities she would have and the many people she could help. *Mom'll be so disappointed if I get married!*

Married! Me married? To Brandon? Will Brandon marry me? Do I want to marry him? Somebody told her he took the girl from Monroe to the last basketball game.

Brandon had warned her to take precautions, but she didn't know how without someone finding out. Besides, she never planned for it to happen. It just did!

Lisa's stomach was churning. She dropped her head back on her arms. What could she do?

The study-hall bell rang and Lisa went unprepared to algebra class. But her mind was made up. She would have to talk to Brandon soon.

3

$\mathcal{T}$alking to Brandon wasn't easy. Lisa was both angry with him and afraid of his charm at the same time. For six weeks she had always been looking somewhere else if he glanced her way. The very sight of him was like a punch in the stomach. Besides, he had been avoiding both homeroom and study hall.

Finally one morning she looked up and Brandon was coming down the aisle toward his seat. Her stomach turned over, but she knew she had to grab the chance. She let her eyes meet his and attempted a smile that she felt freeze on her face. Kevin hadn't come in yet, and Brandon slid down into Kev's seat.

"Hey, Babe, good to see you smile," Brandon said. "Did you ever get things straightened out at home?"

No thanks to you, she snapped silently as she answered, "Oh, sure." She hoped she sounded casual.

"Parents think you're old enough to start dating yet?"

" 'Fraid not, but I'm hoping we can get together again soon," Lisa answered.

"Hey, I'd like that!" Brandon's eyes drifted from Lisa's face down her body as far as the desk would let him look. She felt sick to her stomach even as her pulse quickened. *Is he the same with the girls from Monroe?* she wondered.

"I'm staying after school for help with algebra. I don't have to be home any special time. Could you meet me for a little bit . . . get out of track a while?" Lisa forced herself to ask him. Her parents knew too well she was having trouble with algebra and had told her to ask for help.

"Like an hour or so? We can ride out to that back-road spot we found last winter."

"I can't be too long," Lisa continued, "but we might at least make some plans." *Let him make what he wants of that,* she thought.

Brandon winked at her as Kevin came in and Brandon moved to his own seat. "How about 4:30, at my car, okay?"

———

Brandon's car was parked near the spot where he was practicing shot put. Lisa stood by it and watched in fascination as Brandon heaved the weight. He turned unseeing toward her, thrust the ball up beside his ear, and whirling around with a shout, straightened his arm above his head and hurled the shot into the air. The gleam of his muscles in the sunlight made Lisa think of the pictures of Greek statues in her history book.

Todd Putnam measured the distance Brandon had thrown it.

"Hey, that's your best yet," Todd called. "See if you can do it again."

"Not now. I'm taking a break," Brandon said,

picking up a towel and wiping his face and hands.

Lisa heard Todd laugh as Brandon strode toward her.

"Car's open. Get in," Brandon said. "We'll go to our own special place."

Lisa didn't want to go for a ride with him, but neither did she want to talk in the school yard with people watching. It was only a couple of miles to their parking place.

In the early spring sunlight the dirt road seemed very exposed, with no sheltering leaves on the trees. Lisa was glad Brandon wouldn't attempt anything now.

Brandon drove to the spot where apple trees paraded over the hill on one side and a thicket of wild crab apple hedged the other. She had never been here in daylight before, and never realized how lonely it was with only one farmhouse in the distance.

As Brandon turned off the ignition and slid over beside her, she shivered. She observed the ripple of his hard muscles as he put his arm around her. She leaned her face on his bare shoulder to escape his kiss. A tingling sensation went through her anyway. The muscle under his smooth skin was as stimulating as a kiss. She pulled abruptly away from him, surprised at her own resistance. *Why, oh, why didn't I resist before?* she moaned inside. *Why did I ever let this happen?* A crow cawed in the thicket.

"Hey, where's my sweetheart?" Brandon chided, moving closer to her.

In one burst of courage, Lisa turned her face to his. "I think I'm pregnant," she announced.

He could not have looked more shocked if she had punched him. Lisa turned and stared into the dim thicket as he drew away from her and slumped against the door on his side.

"Caw! Caw! Caw!" The harsh cry of the crow penetrated the closed car.

Lisa began to think time had stopped, but then Brandon straightened. "I thought you were smarter than that. Didn't you ever hear of the pill?" His voice rose as he talked. "I might have known. I suppose you're just too goodie-goodie for that."

The crow flew from the thicket and lighted on a branch of an apple tree close by. "Caw! Caw! Caw!" Its cry beat on Lisa's ears.

Suddenly all was silent. The bare branches of the apple tree wove shadows over the car, and the gloom of the thicket seemed to engulf Lisa. The crow studied the car and flapped away. Lisa could hear her heart beating in her ears.

Into the eternity of silence she whispered, "What are we going to do?"

The crow cawed in the distance.

Finally Brandon spoke again slowly, "I . . . we can't get married."

"We can't get married," Lisa quietly echoed.

"Well, we can't!" Brandon shouted.

"We can't?" Lisa's voice was flat.

"I've got to finish school. I can't keep a wife and a . . ." His voice trailed off.

"I was going to be a nurse," Lisa said and heard the catch in her own voice.

The spring sun shining into the car made it stifling hot. Lisa rolled her window down. The smell of the damp woods came into the car. She could hear the crow again farther away. Brandon didn't want to marry her. It was her problem. She had known all along how it would be, after the night he had left her to face her dad alone. Why did she tell him?

"There is a way out," Brandon spoke at last.

A cold breeze blew from the woods into the car. Somehow she knew what he was going to say before he said it. She shivered. It was in the news all the time, but she hadn't paid much attention. It was a way out. The only way things could be the same again . . . or could they ever be the same?

"Do your parents know?" he asked.

When she shook her head no, Brandon went on, "You could have an abortion."

Her teeth were chattering now. Before she answered she turned her attention to winding the shiny knob that would crank the window back up and shut out the cold air.

Abortion? What did it really mean? Somehow they made you have a period again. You weren't pregnant anymore. What a relief that would be! Who would do it? What did they do? Did it hurt? How could they pay for it? Questions flooded in. If it hurt, she would have to endure it. Escape. That was all that mattered.

"How?" Lisa asked.

Brandon had an answer, "My mom goes to a specialist up in Donaldstown. I heard her say he does abortions. She had to have some kind of surgery, and she said he was real good. He treated her so nice she said it was worth the trip. I know where it is 'cause I took her up once."

"Do you think he'd help me?" Lisa was anxious to talk now, and all the questions came tumbling out.

Bit by bit they worked out a plan. Brandon would make the call. His mom would never notice another long-distance charge from that number. He'd make an appointment for late morning or early afternoon so they could go during school hours. They'd have to skip school and write each other's excuses. Brandon had some money saved from his job last summer and Lisa had some baby-sitting money. Maybe it would be enough.

As they drove back to the school, Lisa felt a faint sense of relief, but as she walked home alone, each step seemed to raise another question. What if the doctor wouldn't see them? What if they didn't have enough money? What if they couldn't get an appointment at the right time? How much would it hurt? Other things began to crowd in too. More deceit. More lies to her mom. She hated it! It had been so hard to face her mother and lie about the times she had sneaked off with Brandon.

Then her mind began to play tricks on her. She had the strange sensation that someone was walking beside her. Someone she refused to look at or name. She began to run.

When she slowed down, out of breath, the childhood game "Step on a Crack, Break Your Mother's

Back" came to her rescue. She blotted out everything else by avoiding cracks the rest of the way home. She didn't want to break her mother's back. Lisa refused to think about her mother's heart.

4

A cold spring rain chilled Lisa as she climbed into Brandon's car in the school parking lot. She was going for an abortion. Somehow Brandon had arranged everything, and they were leaving first thing on this rainy morning for Donaldstown, a drive of an hour and a half.

As they drove out of town, the side windows glazed with steam and raindrops splattered like tears on the windshield. *This can't be for real,* Lisa thought, concentrating on the alternating shine of the wet window and its frosting over with raindrops. The wipers clacked back and forth: clear, unclear; clear, unclear. Like her mind. She knew what she must do, but could she? Should she?

The wipers banged in her head: *I know. I don't know. I know. I don't know. I have to go through with this. I can. I can't. I can. I can't.*

"I got Mom to pack an extra big lunch today. There's enough for you too." Brandon broke into her thoughts with the first words since they had started.

Lunch. Ugh! How could he think about lunch?

"I don't want any lunch," Lisa said, disgusted.

31

"Why not? Everything should be over by lunch-time. I'll bet you'll be hungry."

"More likely I'll be sick."

"Naw, there's nothing to it."

"What do you know about it?" Lisa challenged.

"Coach had a pile of paperbacks on human sexuality in his office. I picked one up and flipped through it. He told me they're for the last nine weeks of health class. So then I asked, casual like, 'Are we going to learn about contraceptives and abortion and all that stuff?' Then I asked how they did abortions anyhow."

"How could you? He'll figure out you were asking for me. Was anyone else around?"

"Well, yah, some of the guys were standing there. But nobody thought anything of it. They were all interested and started asking questions too," Brandon tried to reassure her.

Lisa wasn't reassured. She remembered Todd's laugh when she and Brandon drove off last week. Everyone'll be talking. They'll think I'm awful.

A wave of nausea swept over her. She had begun to feel that way in the mornings lately. She was often afraid she might vomit, and that her mom would hear her and start asking questions. The last few school days she had managed to spend so much time doing her hair that she didn't have time to eat before dashing out the door, and on weekends no one paid much attention to breakfast.

Her mother's face rose between her and the windshield wipers. She had caught Lisa at the door that morning and sent her off with a swat on the backside for not having time to eat the egg she'd prepared, and a kiss to go with her usual wish, "Have a good day." Lisa had juggled her schoolbooks and clutched her purse tightly to her side for fear it might spill out her savings. The purse was stuffed with dollar bills from her baby-sitting, as well as the money Grandma Carson had given her for Christmas.

Her dad had promised to pay the balance on a 14-k gold class ring if she could save $50. She had, but it wasn't easy because she loved to go with Debbie to the mall on Saturdays and shop. She knew her parents didn't approve, but it made her feel more accepted by her friends to be wearing what everyone else was. That's why she wanted a gold ring. It was the "in" thing. Would she ever be able to save enough for it now?

"Did you find out what it costs?" she asked.

"Nope. Forgot. I was too busy talking the nurse into giving you an early appointment. She wanted to make it next month. I told her it couldn't wait."

"Did you tell her why?"

Brandon was picking up speed as he swung onto the Interstate. When he splashed into the lane of traffic he answered, "Not exactly. I just said you were having trouble with your periods and it was urgent."

The nurse probably guessed, Lisa thought ruefully. *But she'll have to know when I get there. I hope Mom doesn't find out. She can't ever know.*

A passing truck blinded them in an upside-down waterfall, and Lisa remembered the tears that blinded her at her mom's kiss that morning. Lisa had given her a quick hug with her free arm, hiding her face over her mom's shoulder, and then hurried out the door, hoping she wouldn't see the tears.

Her mother had told her she would have Lisa's Easter dress ready to fit after school today. At least she hadn't changed size so far, and after this trip she'd be able to wear it for sure.

For your funeral, maybe, a voice mocked inside. That cold hand gripped her stomach again.

"Brandon, is it safe?" Her voice faltered.

Brandon glanced at her, took his right hand from the steering wheel, and patted her on the knee.

"Hey, don't be scared. There's nothing to it. They don't cut or anything like that. It's just a suction thing, sort of like what the dentist puts in your mouth when he fills a tooth. No way can it be dangerous." His voice seemed overconfident.

That's easy for you to say; you're not the one who's going to be operated on, Lisa thought. She pulled away from Brandon, crowding as close to the door on her side as she could get, shivering in the warm car. The wipers banged on: *I can. I can't. I can. I can't.* Then suddenly they seemed to be saying, *I think I can. I think I can. I think I can.* Lisa heard her mother's voice reading aloud *The Little Engine That Could.* For a second she was nestled at her mother's side on the sofa in the den as the story unfolded in her mind. The Little Engine was carrying Christmas toys to the boys and girls on the other side of the mountain. *I'm carrying something, too,* she shuddered—*a boy or girl who will never have any Christmas toys.* She thrust the unwelcome thought from her, concentrating on the wipers. *I think I can. I must for Mom and Dad's and Jenny's sake. I can't disgrace them.*

She stared at the wipers. Somewhere deep inside a small voice whispered, "What an awful secret you'll have to carry all your life." *I think I can. I think I can.*

"I can't! I can't!" another voice cried.

She stirred from her trance as at last a green sign with white letters flashed overhead proclaiming DON-ALDSTOWN, Next Four Exits. Brandon was pulling into the exit lane. A building with a tall smokestack that identified it as a hospital loomed up through the misty rain. Lisa's teeth began to chatter in the steaming car, and she crossed her arms over her stomach, which had begun to churn badly.

I can't be sick now. She fought off the nausea with clenched teeth. *I can't vomit. There's nothing in my stomach,* she told herself. But she retched helplessly as they turned toward the hospital.

"Hey, you all right?" Brandon sounded worried, but he was occupied with the traffic on the busy street.

Getting past the hospital helped a little. Soon the street widened and they were in what had once been a fashionable neighborhood. Just past a big old house, which was now the Red Cross headquarters, they turned into a drive that led behind a two-story medical building. Several doctors were listed on the sign in the front, and Lisa wondered vaguely which one she was to see.

Brandon slowed to check the sign. "Dr. Hackett. That's it."

As Brandon wheeled into a parking place, Lisa fought down the bitter taste of fear in her mouth. She had a great urge to jump out of the car and run as fast as she could, to run and run and run until she dropped and never got up anymore. *If I run up the street in the rain* . . . She could almost hear brakes screeching . . . no. Brandon slammed his door.

She couldn't run away, or go into the doctor's office. She sat frozen as stiff as a goldfish she had once seen someone dig out of an ice-covered pond. A cold rain was blowing into her face. Brandon was standing by her open door under the shadow of a big umbrella.

"Hey, come on. It's not that bad," he was saying in his most cheerful voice.

He reached in, tugging gently on her arm. His touch thawed her enough so she could move. Gulping down her fear, she climbed mechanically out of the car. Brandon pulled her under the umbrella and, putting his arm around her, swept her toward a dark wooden door.

"It won't be long now, Babe," he said, pushing the door open for her.

Just inside the door a violent intestinal cramp caught Lisa and she almost doubled over. She glanced quickly around the waiting room. There it was, the door marked "Ladies." The nurse behind the glass panel was looking at her expectantly, but Lisa didn't have time for her now.

Lisa stumbled into the restroom where she alternated between the toilet and the sink. Her knees wobbled and her insides were empty. She trembled with weakness. Just as a woman in a white uniform stepped into the small room everything went black.

The next thing Lisa saw was white squares with black holes in them. The woman in white was holding something under Lisa's nose that made her feel as if the top of her head was coming off. Ammonia. Lisa reached up to push the offending smell away, and the nurse quickly withdrew the broken capsule. Lisa struggled to sit up. The nurse put a restraining hand on her shoulder.

"Just lie still for a bit. If you try to sit up too soon, you may pass out again." Her voice was kind.

Lisa closed her eyes again, even the effort to move had sent a black wave surging over her.

"I'll be back in a few minutes. You'll feel better, and then we can talk," the nurse said and left her.

Lisa opened her eyes and lay staring at the black dots in the ceiling; one, two, three, four . . . she was detached from her body, floating up into a black dot. Maybe it's over. No, it isn't. She was sad and relieved at the same time. She closed her eyes and let the blackness swirl behind them. She sensed a presence in the room. Was she asleep? She wasn't sure. She opened her eyes and saw the nurse standing over her. Lisa's hands and feet were icy and her teeth began chattering.

"Have you ever passed out before?" the woman asked, lifting Lisa's cold hand in her warm one and gently massaging Lisa's fingers.

Lisa shook her head and through clenched teeth whispered, "I'm scared."

"We get a lot of frightened girls in here. You don't need to be. We're here to do everything we can to help you. You've missed a period? You want to answer a few questions for me?" The nurse stroked Lisa's arm with her other hand, relaxing her enough so that she could talk.

"When did you have your last period?" the nurse asked.

Lisa realized now what an attractive young woman this was and noted the name tag on her pocket: Ms. Lindsey.

Lisa glanced up at the dotted ceiling again.

"I can't remember for sure. I've never paid much attention to dates before, but I think it was before Lincoln's birthday." Her teeth had stopped chattering, but her feet were still cold.

"And now it's early April. If you're pregnant, it would make you about six or seven weeks. That's a good time to remove the product of conception," Ms. Lindsey stated.

Product of conception? Lisa had never heard that term. It sounded as if she were a factory—a baby factory.

"There's only one thing," the nurse hesitated, and Lisa turned her head to look at her questioningly. "How old are you?"

"Fifteen."

Ms. Lindsey frowned. "I was afraid of that. Dr. Hackett won't do abortions on girls under eighteen without a parent's consent. Do yours know about it?"

Lisa looked back at the black holes and saw instead her mother's face. She began shivering again.

"They don't, do they?" The nurse knew the answer. "I can understand that you don't want them to know, but abortion is such a controversial issue that this state requires at least one parent give consent. Dr. Hackett insists teenagers tell their parents first." Her voice was gentle, but final. She went on, "It's better that way. You really shouldn't try to handle this alone. You need your family's backing in case anything should go wrong. It rarely does, but just in case. Even more important is the emotional support they can give. I know you think your mother will be very angry with you, and she probably will be, at first. But usually in the end a girl's mother is her best friend at a time like this. We've seen it happen over and over. You have to cry a little, or maybe even a lot, and your mother should be there to comfort you."

Lisa was counting black holes again: *one, two, I can't tell my mother; three, four, she'll die; five, six, or kill me. . . . How could Mom take it? The whole family would be disgraced. And the people at the church, what if they found out? Would her parents be able to stay there? They've gone there all their lives. It's home to them. And me, too.*

"Honey, you go home and think about it. You'll see we're right. You'll find the courage to tell them. We'll make an appointment for you for next week. We don't want you to put it off too long. If you do, we can't do it in the office. You'll have to go to the hospital."

Lisa found herself back in the waiting room clutching an appointment card in her hand. Brandon was beaming at her.

"Hey, that didn't take long," he said as they went out.

"They didn't do it," Lisa said flatly.

Brandon stopped in the midst of trying to put up the umbrella and stood there with the rain beating down on him.

"They didn't do it?" he asked, tension hardening his face.

"Come on. Let's get in the car," Lisa said quietly. "I'll tell you what happened."

When she had finished her story, Brandon asked, "Is this one of the states where that's the law?"

"Yeah, I guess," Lisa mumbled, leaning her damp head against the back of the car seat. "Let's go back to school. I can't think about it anymore now."

5

Actually Lisa thought of little else than what to do about her pregnancy. Could she tell her mother? No! The answer was always the same. But if she didn't, the doctor wouldn't do the abortion. It was like the circular cage she had for a hamster one time. You kept going round and round and didn't get anywhere. Mom's dear face. It would be easier to spit at her than for Lisa to tell her she was pregnant. But her mom must be getting suspicious. Breakfast became more impossible each morning. Lisa spent more and more time dressing. What could she do?

A few mornings later she caught Brandon outside homeroom and they ducked out to his car. "Tomorrow's the day I'm supposed to take Mom with me to the doctor."

"Have you told her?" Brandon demanded.

"I can't. I just can't." Lisa fought back tears. A school bus was unloading. She couldn't let anyone see her crying.

"I've got some news. Have you had health yet this week?" Brandon asked.

"No, why?" Lisa was puzzled until she remembered about the booklets on human sexuality that Bran-

41

don had mentioned. What had he learned? Did it tell you how to do an abortion? Maybe she could do it herself. It would be dangerous, but anything would be better than telling her mother.

"Coach began our sex education," Brandon said with a smirk, but went on in a more serious vein, "I jumped ahead and asked about state laws. I found out you do need parental consent here, but 200 miles from here they'll do it without your parent's permission."

"Two hundred miles?" It sounded like a continent away. They couldn't do that in a school day.

"That's not so bad," Brandon said. "You can tell your mom you're going to a girlfriend's overnight, and we can drive down some Friday."

"Can't we go this week?"

"No way. Track season starts this Friday."

"What about next week?"

"Don't worry. There's no big hurry. Maybe you'll still have a period or something. Nobody can tell anything to look at you. We'll take care of it before it shows." Brandon assured her.

Lisa and Brandon both glanced at her stomach, which was as flat as ever, probably flatter since she had been eating so little.

Maybe Brandon was right. Maybe it would be a good idea to wait. Maybe there wasn't any hurry. She'd try not to think about it for a while.

On the other hand, the sooner she could get it over with, the better. What a relief it would be. How she dreaded the abortion. Like a visit to the dentist, she didn't want to go, but she didn't want to put it off either. It was bound to hurt.

"Please, Brandon, try to get away next Friday for sure."

Before it shows. The words lingered in her mind as they scurried to beat the late bell to homeroom. *Before it shows*. She slid into her seat. Maybe she wouldn't be able to get near her desk when it showed. Everyone would know she was pregnant.

When did it show? How much time did they really have before it showed? It. What was "it"? The question demanded an answer.

It would be a baby—hers and Brandon's. Something neither of them had planned on when they were messing around. A real live baby! A vision of her cousin Cora's baby leaped into her mind. She remembered how Ellen had snuggled against her when Cora let her hold the baby, and how soft her downy head was as Lisa brushed it with her lips. This in me could be like Ellen. For the first time the picture became clear to her. Black wings beat it back. Not now. It wasn't like that now. A bell rang. Homeroom was over and she wasn't even ready for history class this morning. She couldn't seem to concentrate on any of her studies anymore.

Second period was Lisa's health class. Today Coach Wilkins handed out the paperback books that Brandon had referred to. When it was laid on the desk, Lisa leafed eagerly through it. There were sketches of the reproductive system that she had seen before in a book her mother had given her to read years ago.

"These books are not to leave the class," the coach

announced. "If there are any questions about them, your parents are free to come in to see them. These are new this year, and I feel they are very well done."

Just then Lisa came on a series of diagrams that made her cheeks hot. *How stupid to be embarrassed now,* she thought. I should have been embarrassed before, but then it was dark. If she and Brandon had gone out in the daylight, could it have made any difference? She didn't know. She only wished she didn't know as much as she already did.

"Next week we're going to have two speakers in," Coach Wilkins was announcing. "It's a little bit early in the course, but it was the only time they could fit it into their schedules in the same week, and I'd like you to get both sides of the issue close together. Tuesday we'll have a Pro-Choice speaker, and next Thursday a woman from a Pro-Life group will speak and show a film. Today I'm going to give you a vocabulary list that you can look up either in this book or a dictionary, or you can answer from your own knowledge. Get pencil and paper."

Lisa flipped open her yellow tablet and poised her pencil. The list he wrote on the board ranged from technical terms for the reproductive organs through contraceptive devices and on to abortion methods. The only way Lisa knew was because each part of the list was categorized. The abortion category ran: suction curettage, sharp curettage, dilatation and evacuation, intrauterine saline, and prostaglandin injection. She shivered as she copied the big words from the board.

As soon as he gave them time to begin working on

the definitions, as irresistibly as a child to a mud puddle, she was drawn to look these up first. She read:

"Suction Curettage. The cervix, the opening into the womb, is dilated. A small tube is inserted through the cervix and, by suction, the uterus is gently emptied." *Suction? Gentle? Sounds like a vacuum cleaner for my insides. How strange that'll feel, but maybe it won't hurt after all.*

"Sharp Curettage (D & C). The cervix is dilated and the uterus is cleaned by gently scraping with a spoon-shaped instrument, the curette." *Sharp. Sounds like digging for a splinter. Gentle? Maybe, but probably no worse than having a tooth pulled. Bad enough.*

"Dilatation and Evacuation (D & E). This is a combination of both suction and sharp curettage techniques. There is a growing acceptance of this technique after the first twelve weeks in reaction to evidence that it is safer for the woman than intrauterine instillation." *Twelve weeks? What am I? Seven or eight now. Intrauterine instillation? Oh, that's the next one.*

"Intrauterine Saline or Prostaglandin Injection or Instillation. Salt or prostaglandin solution is injected into the amniotic fluid." *Whatever that is, must be water in the uterus.*

Lisa had never given her uterus much thought, though she guessed the word had been used in the book her mother had given her to read when her periods started. It had also explained how you got pregnant, but she hadn't paid much attention to that either. She was only eleven and, like Peter Pan in the childhood storybooks, didn't want to grow up.

She looked back at the page where she left off: "Salt or prostaglandin injection induces miscarriage usually within 12 to 14 hours."

She couldn't be away that long. That must be when you have to go into the hospital. She'd have to go before twelve weeks when they could still stick something into her uterus and either pull or scrape it out.

"It." The thought of Ellen haunted her.

Another thought crowded in. Dilate the cervix— the opening, the hole that went into the uterus. Dilate? Would it hurt much? Was it like dilating the eyes with drops? That didn't hurt. Then Lisa thought about the cramping she sometimes experienced when she occasionally passed a small blood clot. Did it hurt because it was pushing through the cervix, dilating it? A new idea. If so, it would hurt to force a tube in.

How did they do it? Did they give them Novocain like a dentist? So many questions. Maybe the book had more answers. But she wasn't allowed to take it from the class, and she wouldn't dare ask special permission. She didn't want the coach to know how interested she was. She flipped quickly through the book, but could find nothing about how the cervix was dilated. Drops, like eye drops, she hoped. One thing was sure. She couldn't do it herself.

Nausea swept over her again. She had to get to the restroom. Coach Wilkins looked at her with concern as she hurried to his desk and asked permission to leave.

In the little cubicle she retched and retched, but nothing came up. Finally the nausea subsided and she crept back into the classroom just as the period was ending.

The coach stopped her as she passed his desk. "Are you sick? You look awfully white. Do you want a pass for the nurse's office?"

"No, I'm okay," she answered lamely. How nice it would be to tell Coach everything. But she didn't dare. She and Brandon would handle it, but it had to be soon. If they were going out of state, there would be plans to make, and risks. She hadn't seen much of Debbie lately outside school, but she'd have to pretend to go to her house, though she couldn't tell her either. No one must ever know. *If no one knows, it will be as if it never happened.*

But it was happening. Something was happening right now inside her, in her uterus. "It" was growing.

Lisa retrieved her books and wandered into the hall. She had the feeling that nothing was quite real anymore—nothing except what was going on inside her. It had to end. Soon.

Debbie overtook her. "What's the matter with you?" she wanted to know. "You look awful."

Lisa had been trying to avoid her friend for the past few days. She couldn't think of anything to say until this was over.

"I'm okay," Lisa insisted, then added, "Just a touch of flu."

"Don't you think you ought to go home?" Debbie was concerned.

"No." Lisa shook her head decisively. "I'm better now." She joined her friends in science class.

After school Lisa was waiting for Brandon as he came out of the locker room dressed in his track suit.

"I've got to talk to you," she said, grabbing his arm.

He pushed her hand away. "I don't have time now, but if you can wait, I can take a break later."

When he joined her in his car, she asked him to drive out into the country, but he refused. "I don't have that kind of time today. Tomorrow's our first track meet."

"That's what I want to talk about." Lisa was determined to have it out. "You'll have to miss the meet. I can't wait any longer. Everyone's getting suspicious. Coach and Debbie both asked me today if I was sick, and Debbie wanted me to go home.

"I am sick, and I can't go home. I'm afraid someone'll send me to the nurse like the coach wanted to, and the nurse'll call Mom. We've got to get this over with before someone guesses what's wrong."

Brandon gave her a cool, appraising look. "You don't look bad."

"It's in the morning that I'm having trouble. You know what happened when you took me to the doctor. What if I faint in school?"

"You only fainted because you were scared. Besides, how am I going to take you on a 200-mile trip if you get sick and pass out on me?" He became defensive.

"I'll be okay. I promise. I know what they're going to do now."

"Then you'll be all right until I can go."

"You won't take me tomorrow?"

"You don't think I've worked for months to get ready for the track season only to miss the first meet. Forget it!"

"But what about me? Think how I feel. I'm the one people are staring at and asking questions about. I'm the one who's going to have a baby." She stopped, appalled. It was the first time she had said it aloud.

Baby. The word floated in the silence and seemed to echo over and over inside the closed car as if it were trapped like the child growing inside her. *Baby, baby, baby.* Was it only in Lisa's head? *Baby.* Ellen's soft, downy head. . . .

"I know all that," Brandon said irritably. "But what about me? I only have these few weeks to make it in track season, and if I miss a meet I miss my chance to set a record. I'm not going to miss any track meets. I'll take you when they're over, unless—"

"Unless what?" Lisa asked eagerly.

"Unless you can figure out some way we can go during the week. We could come back the same day, but we'd be awful late getting home."

"My parents'll never let me stay out anywhere on a school night."

"Then I guess it's your problem," Brandon said. He climbed out of the car, slammed the door, and jogged back to practice.

Frustrated, fearful, and hoping to reach the girls' room before she burst into tears, Lisa jumped out of the car and ran into the building just as Coach Wilkins came out of his office. Dashing blindly down the hall, Lisa collided with him. She tried to sidestep him, but he caught and held her. Overwhelmed by his strong but gentle grip, she sobbed into his sweatshirt.

When the storm was over he let her go. Looking up at him, Lisa could see the honest concern in his blue eyes. He was a tall, rugged man in his early thirties, a man she could trust.

"Come on into my office and tell me all about it," he said, moving to the door and pushing it open. Like a sleepwalker she obeyed automatically. It would be good to finally talk to someone.

The story poured out. He listened gravely, asking only an occasional question to encourage her.

"You don't want your parents to know?"

"No. They must never find out."

"You're sure you want an abortion? Absolutely sure?"

Lisa wavered at the word absolutely. She knew absolutely she didn't want to be pregnant, that she didn't want her parents to know. Absolutely an abortion?

"There's no other way," she mumbled, defeated.

"Brandon's right about one thing. It can wait a little while yet. Why don't you hold off until you've heard both sides of the abortion issue presented in health class. In the meantime, you could get some medicine for your upset stomach over the counter in the drugstore. There are several things that might help, anything that coats the stomach."

"You really think they have something that'd make me feel better?"

"It's worth a try."

Lisa got up to go. "Thanks," she said, shifting her

books from her lap to her arm and shouldering her purse.

"And, Lisa, don't worry. Your secret's safe with me," the coach promised. Lisa knew it was.

6

$\mathcal{S}$econd period Tuesday morning Lisa busied herself piling her books on the floor under the seat ahead
of her and opening her notebook. Coach Wilkins had
arranged for all the health classes to meet together for
the talk by the Pro-Choice speaker. Brandon came in
and sat down beside her. She didn't appreciate it, but
she managed a smile. She hoped the talk might convince Brandon of the need for action. Debbie and Lane
were in the same row with them.

Lisa had been feeling better in the mornings since
her talk with the coach. She wasn't sure if it was the
medicine or the talk that had helped most.

Coach Wilkins came out now onto the platform and
introduced the Reverend Crane, a thin-faced Presby-
terian minister. A minister in favor of abortion? It surprised her. Lisa didn't think a minister would be. But
why not? She didn't have time then to think about the
question.

Rev. Crane launched into a tale of a thirteen-year-
old girl who was pregnant by her uncle. Then he was
on to another story of a twelve-year-old who had been
raped by her mother's boyfriend, and another about a
pregnant retarded child. No one knew who the father

was. Lisa was astounded. How could such ugly things happen? She didn't really want to know about them.

In each case, Rev. Crane said, the girls had been brought to the counseling center by their mothers to have an abortion. Lisa felt relieved for each of them.

But what about me? she wondered. *No one forced me into this mess. I got myself into it.*

Rev. Crane went on to speak about girls like Lisa who got pregnant by a boyfriend at an inconvenient time. *Now I'll get it,* she thought.

"Abortion is the sensible way out," Rev. Crane asserted, again surprising Lisa.

Tracy Flemming, one of the girls usually in Lisa's health class, shot up her hand.

"What about the baby? Isn't that taking a life?" she challenged.

The man answered blandly, "No one has agreed when life begins. If an abortion is done early, it's only a clump of cells. If it's done later as it was with the retarded girl, isn't everyone better off? What kind of a life would her child have?"

You could hear the quaver in Tracy's voice as she answered, "God can take care of her baby. God gives life, and God should be the one to take it."

Lisa felt nervous for Tracy even as she found herself agreeing with her. She waited anxiously for Rev. Crane's answer.

"Don't you think you're putting a lot on God?" he answered. "God has given us all this knowledge and we should use it."

Right, God has given knowledge. Lisa latched onto that idea.

Tracy was about to answer when the coach broke in, "We aren't here to argue. You'll hear the other side Thursday. Please let Rev. Crane finish his presentation."

Rev. Crane went on to discuss the Supreme Court ruling on legalized abortion and what he considered to be the dangerous way Pro-Life groups were pushing for an amendment to the Constitution that would take away the woman's right to make a choice about what happened in her own body. Such a law would bring back the era of back-room abortions with all kinds of infection that led to the death of many women, he warned. He concluded by stressing that women should have a choice, and restated the reasonableness of abortion when a girl wasn't ready to have a baby.

As an afterthought, he warned them that while abortions can be done legally up to seven months, "It's much safer the earlier it's done."

Lisa had an overwhelming desire to nudge Brandon, but she was afraid someone might notice. Instead, she kept her head bent over her notebook and looked at him out of the corner of her eye. He seemed to be listening, but would it do any good? She determined to wait until after the Pro-Life speaker on Thursday before she bugged him again to take her Friday.

Going out of the auditorium, she overheard Tracy saying to another girl, "God put the Tree of Knowledge in the Garden of Eden too, but Adam and Eve weren't supposed to eat from it." Lisa winced.

———————

Thursday, Brandon didn't sit by her. Instead, he sat with Lane and Todd in the back row. Debbie came in and sat beside Lisa.

"What's the matter with those guys? Guess they can't take it," she said.

"It might be embarrassing," Lisa commented, wondering why she didn't cut class. She wasn't sure she wanted to hear the Pro-Life speaker.

"That's right, we see a film today," Debbie said as she noticed the screen pulled down on the stage. "But it'll be dark. Why should anybody be embarrassed?"

"I don't know, but I'm just as glad not to sit with the guys," Lisa said.

They stopped talking as the coach led an attractively dressed, dark-haired woman about the same age as Lisa's mother onto the platform, and introduced Mrs. Neller.

She began by saying that everyone was stressing freedom and rights today. Then, raising her arms and stretching them out at shoulder height, she swung around, twirling over to the coach and stopping just short of hitting him in the face.

"What's wrong?" she asked innocently as the coach jerked his head back.

Everyone laughed as she turned back to the students. "I have a right to swing my arms around, don't I? It's a free world. Nobody can tell me I can't."

"But you better not hit me," Coach Wilkins cracked.

"I won't," she promised, coming back to center stage.

"My rights end where Mr. Wilkins' nose begins," she addressed the class. "It seems as if everyone has rights today except the unborn child. No one pays any attention to his or her nose. Today we're going to see what this unprotected miniature human being looks like and let you decide if he or she—and we can tell early which it is—deserves any rights. You're going to witness the development of a baby from a tiny cell until it's ready to be born."

Mrs. Neller signaled for the film to begin. The lights went down, film crackled, crosses in circles flashed on the screen, and Lisa watched an egg being fertilized. It divided rapidly into two, four, eight cells, until by the end of the third week the backbone, spinal column, and nervous system were definable and at the fourth week buds for arms and legs appeared. In eight weeks fingers and toes were well begun and by twelve weeks, or just three months, the hands and feet looked almost exactly like Ellen's the first time Lisa saw her.

As the film rolled on, the fetus looked more and more like Ellen, but it was the eight-week pictures that made an indelible impression on Lisa. That's what hers must be, about eight weeks; and if Brandon didn't take her soon, it might even be twelve weeks. By then the eyes, ears, and nose were already in place. A muscle in Lisa's leg jumped, and she shifted quickly so that Debbie wouldn't notice. She could scarcely sit still for the rest of the film.

Finally they showed a baby being born, and something deep inside Lisa responded to the scene. A baby. *My baby. What am I thinking of? My baby. So very much alive. Can I kill my baby?* She felt as if her stomach were full of whole walnuts in the shell and one had stuck in her throat. Her eyes burned and tears ran against her will. How glad she was for the dark as they streamed down her face. *But I've got to stop crying. The film's almost over.* She fumbled for a tissue in her purse and blew her nose.

"Were you crying?" Debbie wanted to know when the lights came on.

"No!" Lisa snapped. "I think I'm allergic to something. Maybe it's the new perfume you're wearing."

Mrs. Neller was on stage again. "If you have any questions, I'll be glad to answer them, but first I have a question for you. When did life begin? The Pro-Choice people claim no one knows when life begins, but after seeing this film, what do you think?"

Before there was any chance to answer or ask other questions, the dismissal bell rang, and it was time for science.

The coach was standing by the door as Lisa straggled out of the auditorium. He stopped her for a second and said quietly, "If you want to talk about anything, I'll be in my office after school."

Brandon was waiting for her in the hall in front of the nurse's office. He was as white as the walls behind him. "We'd better keep that date for Friday," he said.

Lisa looked at him as if she didn't know what he was talking about and walked away.

He sprinted to catch up with her, "Hey, meet me

after school," he commanded as she turned into science class.

She dropped into her seat. Two offers after school: the coach or Brandon. She knew it was a life-and-death choice she was making for the fetus growing inside her.

Mr. Vores, the science teacher, had seen the film too, and everyone in the class wanted to discuss it—except Lisa. She was nauseous again. Could she go to the nurse's office? She noticed when Brandon stopped her that there was no one in her office. Maybe the nurse was visiting another building in the school district and Lisa could have the room to herself. Maybe not. No, she'd better try to hang on here. It would attract less attention. *I didn't eat breakfast, so I can't vomit,* she told herself.

Everyone was surprised at how early a fetus looked like a baby, and all the things it could do—hear, cry, and suck its thumb before it was born—and how early the heart started beating. Lisa's own heart beat faster as she realized that the tiny one inside her had a pulse too. She wanted to shut out the discussion, but she couldn't.

Why did I ever see the film? Why didn't I cut class? Some kids did cut out and go upstreet, usually for cigarettes. Of course, she never did, nor could she have gotten away with it today. She was sure Coach Wilkins was looking for her.

The discussion swirled, and she slumped down in her seat, hoping to be inconspicuous. It seemed to be working, since Mr. Vores didn't call on her. It wasn't necessary. Too many hands were waving for his recognition.

The discussion shifted to abortion, and the weight of opinion ran strongly for it, though some still felt the second speaker was right about when life begins. An argument developed between Sara, who was a strong Catholic, and Allie, who was known to be pretty liberal on all kinds of subjects.

"Nobody's going to tell me what I can do with my body," Allie declared.

"But it's murder," Sara countered.

"Okay. Is it murder?" Mr. Vores interjected. "What about it? When does life begin? That's the big argument."

The class fell silent. Lisa felt as if the question were aimed at her. Mr. Vores' eyes wandered around the room and finally came to rest on her. "Lisa, we haven't heard anything from you today. What do you think?"

The muscle in her leg vibrated uncontrollably. She was glad she was seated, otherwise she might have fallen. Her stomach was in knots. That question had been ringing in the back of her own mind since she had left the auditorium, the question she didn't want to think about.

"I don't know." The steadiness of her own voice surprised her.

"At conception," Sara cut in without being called on.

"It's not a life until it can live by itself outside its mother," Allie came back without being called on either.

"All right, girls," Mr. Vores cut them off. "We're not going to settle this. That's where the debate rages.

It's something about which you have to make up your own minds. We'd better get to our lesson now."

Sara wasn't to be put off, "It is alive from the moment the egg and sperm unite. Before that there isn't human life; after that there is. If things go normally, in nine months a baby will be born. It is alive. Abortion is taking a life."

Mr. Vores nodded thoughtfully and said, "But can it be considered alive when it's still dependent on the mother's bloodstream?"

Sara and Allie were ready to argue more, but Mr. Vores deftly turned them off. However, the argument continued to rage within Lisa.

It's a baby growing in me. It has a right to life. But what about my life? I have a right to life too. It'll ruin my life, Mom's, Dad's, and Jenny's too. She had been over all this before, but the new factor was the baby's life. Could she end it? Was it really murder?

At three o'clock Lisa's steps dragged as she started down the stairs leading into the hall past the coach's office, the gym, and out into the parking lot. She still didn't know if she would stop to see the coach. She wandered slowly down the hall, stopping at the cafeteria door to watch the custodian wield his big mop across the floor. He looked over and smiled, and she pushed herself on down the hall.

"Oh, God, what should I do?" It was the first time she had prayed in months, or was it the first time she had ever really prayed? It seemed then that she was drawn into the coach's office. His strong face lit with a smile as she came in. When she was seated, he asked her what she thought of the presentations, but she didn't answer. She just stared at the floor.

The coach took the initiative. "You know, I have a little girl just starting school, and I pray that God will protect her from what's happened to you. But if she did get into trouble, I'd want to know. I realize how great temptations are today, and I'm going to do everything I can to keep her from them—the same as your parents have tried to do. I'd be hurt and ashamed if she got pregnant, but I would feel even worse if she didn't confide in me. I'll go on loving her no matter what happens. I'm sure your parents would feel the same way. Why don't you tell them so you can work this out as a family?"

Lisa was crying softly now, with her hands over her face.

"Will you do that, Lisa? Will you tell them? I'm sure that's the best thing you can do right now."

Lisa glanced up at him through her tears. "All right," she promised.

7

$\mathcal{D}$inner was over and Mrs. Carson was sitting in the living room hemming Lisa's Easter dress. The lamplight fell in a circle on her efficient hands as she drew the needle through the soft material. Patches, their calico cat, was curled up beside her. Jenny had retreated to her bedroom. She had turned up the stereo, the one she had begged for from her dad for her birthday, as loud as her mother would permit. Mr. Carson was at the store as usual on Thursday nights.

Lisa came into the living room and dropped onto the end of the sofa before her shaking knees gave way. Patches looked up, gave a friendly "meow," and ambled over to her. Lisa lifted her onto her lap and buried her cold hands in Patches' long fur.

"Something wrong?" her mother asked, glancing up. "Have you changed your mind about the length of your skirt?"

"Oh no, it's fine. I really like the dress, and I like Jenny's too, but . . ." Lisa hesitated, then plunged on, "something is wrong. . . . Mom, I haven't had a period since February."

She must have clutched Patches too hard. The cat struggled free and jumped from her lap.

Her mom's hand poised with the needle in midair, then descended in slow motion onto her lap.

"Oh, Lisa," she said, looking at her daughter, eyes dark with dread. "I've been so afraid of this ever since that awful night. You lied to me, didn't you?" Her voice quavered.

Lisa noticed a loose piece of skin by her cuticle and began picking at it. "Yes," she whispered.

"I felt guilty not trusting you, but I was so afraid of this. You're so young. We tried to protect you, but we failed." Her mother's voice broke.

"Oh, Mom, don't blame yourself. It wasn't your fault." Lisa wished she'd yell at her or smack her—anything besides this quiet acceptance.

"I went for an abortion, but the doctor—"

"Abortion!" Her voice rose, then fell away, "Oh, dear God!"

"The doctor wouldn't do it without your permission. Brandon and I were going to go out of state as soon as he could get away, but—"

"Then you didn't have an abortion." Regret and relief seemed mingled in her voice.

Lisa pulled at the flesh on her finger until it began to bleed. She put the finger to her mouth. "No," she mumbled through the salty taste of blood, and looked sideways at her mother, still waiting for an explosion.

She turned from Lisa and pushed herself to her feet by using the arm of the sofa the way Grandma Carson did, a strange action for her mother who always sprang to her feet so lightly. Lisa watched her walk heavily across the room to the kitchen doorway where she stood quietly staring into the darkness. Her voice had a hollow sound when she spoke again.

"I don't know what to say. I'm forced to think the unthinkable. My daughter pregnant . . . not married . . . pregnant, a time that should be one of the happiest in a woman's life . . . my daughter, still a child . . . going to have a baby."

It seemed as if she had almost forgotten Lisa was listening.

"How can it be?" she rambled on. "I've prayed for her to be protected from the temptations of growing up, especially this. Why, dear Lord, why?" She leaned her head against the doorjamb.

Lisa looked at the dress crumpled on the floor where it had fallen from her mother's lap. Lisa bit more skin from her finger. The taste of blood nauseated her.

God gives life. God takes life. Tracy's words resounded in Lisa's head as if in answer.

"Abortion." Her mother turned back to her. "How tempting to escape that way. All over . . . like nothing ever happened. But it would be like Adam and Eve eating the forbidden fruit, then trying to hide from God. They couldn't, and neither can we. No, abortion isn't the answer. The whole creative process is so wonderful that we dare not interfere once it's begun."

"Eating the forbidden fruit." The phrase struck Lisa with a parallel, "Thou shalt not commit adultery," and she had. Her mother was right. She couldn't hide from God by breaking another of His commandments. He also said, "Thou shalt not kill."

"We'll have to tell your father." She seemed to be

thinking of details now. "I'll do it. Why don't you go to your room and try to get your homework done?"

As Lisa ran to the steps, her mother caught her in her arms. "I'm thankful you told me. We'll work this out together. It's not the way we would have planned it, but with God's help we'll see you through." She gave Lisa a quick kiss.

"Thanks, Mom," Lisa gulped. She could scarcely see to stumble up the stairs.

In her room, Lisa sank into her desk chair and dropped her head in her hands. The textbooks lay untouched. At last she got up listlessly, put on her pajamas and, lying down on the bed, listened for her father.

Jenny's stereo had been quiet a long time when the garage door rattled up under Lisa's front bedroom. Her father's car pulled into the garage, the engine stopped, and the door rattled shut. He must have worked on his books after the store closed as he often did. Mom would greet him with a kiss when he came in . . . or would she tonight?

Lisa padded into the carpeted hall. Apparently her mother had gone to wait for him in the family room, the half flight down from the kitchen and behind the garage. If they would come up to the living room, she could hear what they said, but down there voices were muffled. Lisa crept down the half flight to the living room and stepped into the dark kitchen to listen at the stairwell.

"Irene, you look awful. What's wrong?" he asked. Shivering, Lisa pressed her back against the wall to hold herself up. Something furry brushed past her legs in the dark. Patches. She picked her up and cuddled her to try to get warm.

Her mother said, "Lisa thinks she's pregnant."

"Our Lisa? Pregnant?" he gasped. Then his voice rose in anger. "Brandon! That creep! I'll kill him for doing that to my daughter."

Lisa hadn't expected this. She never dreamed he'd blame Brandon instead of her.

"Dave, you don't mean that," she said.

Firm, loud, measured footsteps on the tile floor approached the steps. Lisa dropped Patches and scurried for the bedroom stairs, but the footsteps changed direction, and she eased back to her former position.

"You're right, but he sure deserves a horsewhipping."

"It wasn't all his fault. Lisa went off with him of her own accord. He didn't kidnap her." Her mother's voice had a deep sadness in it.

"He'll have to marry her," her dad declared.

"Oh no! He's only sixteen." She sounded shocked.

"If he's old enough to father a child, he's old enough to be responsible for his action. That's what my father always told me, and he's absolutely right," he stormed. "I'm going to call his father. Brandon's going to face me this time."

Marry Brandon? Call his father? Surely Dad wasn't serious. Before she could move, her father was on the stairs dashing for the kitchen phone. Lisa switched on the light.

"Dad!" she exclaimed as he charged into the room,

his face red with anger, "I can't marry Brandon. Please don't call his parents."

Her father stopped short as she confronted him, gave her a long hard look, and reached for the phone book.

"Danforth. His dad's an insurance agent over in Leedsville? Right?"

Lisa nodded confirmation as her insides froze into a ball of ice while her legs seemed to be melting under her.

Her mother came running up the steps behind him, calling, "Wait, Dave, don't call them yet. Wait until you're calmer."

Her dad found the number and began to dial, but her mother reached the phone and pushed down the switch, breaking the connection. "Please. We need to figure this out ourselves."

"We need to figure it out with Brandon." Undeterred, he lifted her hand firmly from the phone and proceeded to dial.

"Mrs. Danforth?" Lisa heard her father's voice from a long way off. "This is Mr. Carson. I'd like to speak to your husband."

As he listened to her response, a funny look came over his face, the same look he got when he'd just lost a game of chess.

"Oh," he said lamely. Then he seemed to recover his steam and demanded, "Then I'll talk to your son."

Her dad was silent for a little and then snapped, "You can ask *him* what it's about! Tell him I want to see him at our house tomorrow evening at 7:30 without fail. You'd better try to get ahold of his father to come with him."

Her father listened for the answer, then said, "Yes, you may come if you want to. Remember, tomorrow night I want Brandon here."

He dropped the phone back on the hook and announced, "His father left his mother several months ago."

"No wonder he acts like he does. What kind of an example has he had?" her mother said.

Lisa, who had grabbed a stool from the breakfast bar to hold herself up, stood up straight now. "Dad, he knows I'm pregnant. It won't change anything to bring him here. Please don't make him come. He tried to take me for an abortion."

"Abortion? You were going for an abortion without telling your parents?" His jaw that had been set so firmly quivered now.

"But she didn't have it," her mother interjected.

"Why not?" he demanded.

"Because the doctor she went to required parental consent, and now she's changed her mind, haven't you, Lisa?" She asked and answered her question in the same breath.

Have I changed my mind? she wondered. *I guess I have.*

"Abortion." There was a speculative note in her dad's voice. "That would take care of everything."

"Except our conscience," her mom said convincingly. Her dad looked at Lisa, then at her mother, and back to Lisa.

"Go on back to bed. We can't do anything more tonight." He dismissed her without the usual good-night kiss.

Lisa fled to her bed, crawling between two sheets so cold they made her think of the time she had fallen through the ice. Her teeth chattered uncontrollably. She could hear the rise and fall of her parents' voices.

Surely Dad won't make Brandon marry me. She could see Brandon hurling the shot, and visualize his muscles tough as a pile of leather belts lashed together. What might he do to her if he became really angry? She shook so hard the bed nearly quivered.

"I'd rather die now than marry Brandon," she whispered.

No sooner had the thought expressed itself than she knew she didn't want to die. She recalled the terror she had felt as she had fallen through the ice and, cold as she was, the relief that followed when her skates had come to rest in the mud and her shoulders were still above the water that was spreading over the broken ice. She hadn't wanted to die then. She didn't want to die now.

"God, help me. Please help!" The prayer sprang to her lips for the second time that day.

An accusing voice rose within: "Why should God help you when you've turned your back on Him?"

"Because of Jesus," another voice answered. "He died to forgive sins." *But I sinned deliberately. Daddy didn't forgive me. How can God?*

Lisa tossed and turned until her weary body finally overcame her tortured mind and she escaped into sleep.

8

Lisa felt like crawling into the crack between the two cushions on the sofa where she sat as her father admitted a strange man the next evening. Then as she caught the same half-amused look in his blue eyes that she had fallen for in Brandon's, he didn't seem so strange, only now she felt like a piece of merchandise as Brandon's father looked her over.

"Lisa, I can see my son has good taste," Mr. Danforth said after introductions were made.

Lisa straightened abruptly and lifted her chin. At the same time she noted the twitch in her dad's jaw that betrayed anger or disapproval. What would happen? He had been unrelenting in demanding that Brandon come.

"I'm afraid his taste has gotten us all into trouble," Mr. Carson said.

"They aren't here yet, I see," Mr. Danforth said.

"Won't you sit down?" Her mother was the good hostess.

He was barely seated when the bell rang again, and Brandon and his mother arrived. Lisa avoided looking at Brandon, but stared instead at his mother. She had Brandon's rich reddish hair, but her mouth was tight with lines that were not recent and her eyes darted about the room, never seeming to stop long anywhere.

When the formalities were over and everyone was seated, Brandon's dad took the lead, "We've got to decide what to do. Of course there is only one civilized answer."

Cutting off Mr. Danforth, Lisa's dad gave it: "Marriage."

"Brandon can't marry. He's only a baby himself," his mother protested.

"When a boy is old enough to father a child, he's old enough to provide for it," her dad proclaimed.

Mr. Danforth crossed his legs casually and adjusted his pant leg before he answered, "I'm prepared to pay for the best doctor and take care of any recompense for damages, so to speak, within reason," he went on as if Mr. Carson hadn't spoken.

"You think you can buy your way out of this situation?" Mr. Carson's face was red and his jaw twitched harder. "He's in it as much as Lisa. I say he has to marry her."

Brandon laughed a nervous laugh and spoke for the first time, "But, Mr. Carson, you wouldn't want me to marry your daughter if I don't love her, would you?"

Mr. Carson looked from Lisa to Brandon, to his wife, to Mr. Danforth, to Mrs. Danforth who had chosen a seat as far from her husband as possible and looked completely miserable.

"Don't you love her?" It sounded as though the idea had never crossed David Carson's mind.

"No," Brandon said. "I don't love her."

"Why did you do it?" Mr. Carson asked.

"Because she was such a good girl. A challenge." Then that half-amused look came over his face and he added, "It wasn't that hard after all."

Something inside Lisa curled up like a leaf bruised in a hailstorm.

"Get out! Get out of here, all of you!" her dad shouted.

Lisa didn't really see the Danforths leave. She just sat there feeling cold from the inside out. As if in a dream, Lisa could hear her mother crying and saw her sister peeking down from the top of the steps, her eyes wide.

When the door closed Jenny charged down the steps.

"What horrible people!" she cried, throwing herself down on the sofa beside Lisa and flinging her arms around her shoulders. "We love you, Lisa. We love you."

A tiny place inside Lisa began to thaw. Jenny had never before said she loved her. In fact, Lisa often thought Jenny hated her. Following Jenny's lead, her mom and dad crowded around her too.

"Oh, yes, Lisa, we love you too," her mom added.

Lisa's eyes sought her dad's still red face. Could he love her? She had been so bad. How could anyone love her?

Her dad reached down, grabbed her hands, pulled her to her feet and into his arms, "I love you, Lisa. We'll handle this ourselves. I was out of my mind to think of Brandon marrying you."

The hailstones inside melted and washed away in the warmth of the family's love, but nothing was really solved.

When her dad let her go, Lisa asked the question uppermost in her mind: "How will we handle it? I can't go back to school. Everyone'll know."

"Not really. No one that didn't know before," Jenny said. "I'm sure Brandon had to do some bragging about his conquest, but I'll bet he hasn't told them he got you pregnant."

How could Jenny be so smart for only thirteen? Lisa wondered. She was sure she was right as she thought about Todd Putnam's smirk and even the fact that Brandon had known about Todd and her kissing on the bus. How dumb could she have been? She had really been set up. Now she was angry, angry enough to face them all, and she wanted to get even.

"Poor Brandon," her mom said.

"What do you mean 'poor Brandon'?" Lisa turned on her.

"I'm afraid he's already doomed to move from conquest to conquest and will never know a lasting, loving relationship. We need to pray for him."

Lisa was taken aback. Her mom was talking about praying for Brandon when she wanted revenge.

Her mother changed the subject. "I found out about a home for unwed mothers today in the Donaldstown area. I thought it might be easier to spend the last few months of your pregnancy there. It's less than two months until school is out for the summer, and you could drop out for the fall semester. They offer tutoring at the home to keep you up with your class. You could profit from special help."

"That sounds like a good idea." It was news to her dad too.

"But what about after the baby comes?" Lisa asked.

"If you go to the home, you might want to give the baby up for adoption. No one here would ever have to know about it," her mother said gently, and paused, considering for a minute, "or if you want to keep it, I would have to take care of it."

"But you were going to start back into nursing this fall," her father said.

Lisa didn't know that. If anyone had talked about it, she had been too preoccupied with her own problems to hear.

"It can wait, if it has to," her mother said.

"But, Mom, it's your turn to do what you want to do now," Jenny said.

"Lisa needs her education first, especially if she has to raise a child alone," her mother answered.

"Does she have to have the child? Was Brandon's dad right in his implication? Why isn't abortion the answer?" Her father seemed to be questioning within himself. Then he said, "I've been reading through the Gospels again, and it struck me that Christ was characterized by caring about people and their problems. Would it be so terrible to spare everyone more pain?"

"It's taking a life. Can we justify that?" her mother asked.

"It's the coward's way out," Jenny declared, again surprising her sister.

"The Bible has something to say about God's caring for the unborn child too. Jenny, check Psalm 139 for us, will you?" her mother said.

Jenny ran to the kitchen and brought the Bible from the bookshelf under the breakfast bar. She leafed through until she found the psalm and then read: " 'For you created my inmost being; you knit me together in my mother's womb. I praise you because I am fearfully and wonderfully made; your works are wonderful, I know that full well. My frame was not hidden from you when I was made in the secret place. When I was woven together in the depths of the earth, your eyes saw my unformed body. All the days ordained for me were written in your book before one of them came to be.' "

Jenny looked up from the Bible and exclaimed, "Wow! How about that. God forms us in the womb. Of course He does."

"Maybe He's only talking about David," Lisa suggested. "Could God have anything to do with my child who was begun in sin?"

"Those verses are talking about all of us. We believe God has a plan for every life if we let Him take charge," her dad conceded.

"David wasn't a perfect person. In one place he says, 'In sin did my mother conceive me.' We don't have to be perfect for God to care about us. He proved that by sending Jesus. Remember, 'while we were yet sinners, Christ died for us.' " Her mother seemed to read Lisa's thoughts.

"Knit together. That's neat," Jenny said. "We've been learning about chromosomes and genes. That must mean God chooses all the genes and intertwines them to make us what we are."

"Lisa's baby too," her mother added.

"Okay. So maybe the home's the answer for you, Lisa, but we don't have to decide tonight. We'll ride over and look at it sometime soon. Then you can decide." Dad gave Lisa one more hug and left the room.

9

$\mathcal{L}$isa found it easier than she had believed it would be to go back to school for the rest of the term. It gave her a certain satisfaction to ignore Brandon and Todd and say cutting things about them to anyone who would listen. Best of all, she heard that Brandon wasn't doing well in the shot put, and she was glad.

Now school was out for the Easter holiday. Tomorrow was Good Friday, and Lisa found a certain uneasiness growing in herself that was only partly related to her pregnancy. Mom had taken her to a doctor in Leedsville, and he said everything was fine and he would deliver the baby if she decided to have it there. Her nausea improved and so far no one could tell she was pregnant. Next week they would visit the home for unwed mothers and then they would decide, but right now it was something else.

She went to her room early, knowing that tonight was the night she would have to face herself because tomorrow they would be going to Good Friday service and communion. It was communion that worried her. She knew that if she were to take communion, she had to first do some self-examining that she had been avoiding.

She turned to the New Testament and began reading through the gospel story of the crucifixion. There in the middle of it all stood Peter, Peter who denied his Lord, Peter who had promised to die with Jesus. She thought of her own self-assurance when she had been just a little younger, her great confidence when she joined the church that she would always be a good Christian and do what was right. She had felt very secure in her faith that Jesus Christ was her Savior, that He died for her sins, though she had never been greatly troubled by sin.

It was different now. Was it the same with Peter? He had been very sure too, and then he said he didn't know Jesus. She had acted as if she didn't know Jesus either when she gave in to Brandon.

Sliding down to her knees beside her bed, Lisa began to cry great tears of remorse, not because she was pregnant—she had shed enough tears for her own dilemma—but because in a very real sense she had denied her Lord. Everyone had considered her a "good" girl. They knew she tried to do what was right, and now this . . . this was all wrong. It wasn't only her own reputation that was at stake, but what an excuse to ridicule Christians, to ridicule Christ, the way TV shows liked to do. The "good guy" always turned out to be bad. No one needed her example.

As she knelt there she visualized the cross. She could see Jesus with head bent and arms outstretched, suffering there, for her. For the first time in her life she realized what her salvation had cost.

She cried harder and thought about what Peter did.

She remembered he was the first one to enter the tomb, and that Jesus had a very special conversation with him on the shore of Galilee. Jesus asked Peter if he loved Him. *Is He asking me the same question?* she wondered.

Slowly her sobbing subsided. *Do I love Him? Jesus who died for me, for my sins, yes, even this one.* "Oh, Lord, I love you. Please forgive me," she whispered. "Please forgive me."

"Forgive us our debts as we forgive our debtors," the phrase from the Lord's Prayer spoke itself to her mind. "As we forgive." The words sounded over and over as though a record had jammed. *As we forgive.*

She hadn't forgiven Brandon. When Brandon had said she'd been "so easy," she'd vowed she'd never forgive him. Her cheeks burned even now as she remembered. *Does this mean I have to forgive Brandon if Jesus is going to forgive me? Am I asking to be forgiven as much as I forgive? Do I want to be forgiven enough to forgive Brandon?*

"Yes, oh yes," Lisa was praying now. "I'll forgive him, Lord, but you'll have to help. Please, dear Jesus." And even then Lisa knew she would have to apologize to Brandon for the nasty things she'd been saying about him at school. It would be hard, but she knew God would help her.

Her head was buried in her arms and her face crushed into her bed covers. She was looking into total darkness when suddenly that strange feeling she had had a couple of times since she had been pregnant came again, just for an instant. Lisa knew someone was with her and she knew who it was. It was good to stop running from Him.

Tears flowed again, but this time they were tears of joy. Instantly she was free—free of guilt and free of hatred toward Brandon.

"I forgive him," she heard herself speak in the quiet room, and she knew, too, that she herself was forgiven.

As she opened her eyes, she saw her Easter dress hanging on the closet door. For a while Lisa thought her mom would never finish it, but she had. Lisa knew this was a sign that her mother also had forgiven her.

Anxious now for a word of assurance from the Bible, she picked it up and looked for the Twenty-third Psalm. Though she could recite it, she wanted to read again, "The Lord is my shepherd." Instead of the Psalms, the Bible fell open to Isaiah, and a verse in the fortieth chapter leaped out at her. "He tends his flock like a shepherd: He gathers the lambs in his arms and carries them close to his heart; he gently leads those that have young."

"The Lord is my shepherd," she mumbled, and prayed quietly, "Thank you, Lord Jesus. I know you'll be with me in the days ahead and help me to make the right decisions."

With a sense of peace she leafed back to the Twenty-third Psalm and read it through before she turned out the light.

10

$\mathcal{E}$aster was a glorious day, but Monday came and Lisa had to face the problems raised by her pregnancy. With her parents she was on her way to visit the home for unwed mothers. The April sun shone brightly, but Lisa wished it were raining. It would have suited her mood better. Every time she thought of leaving home for a strange place, clouds of gloom descended on her.

She especially hated to leave home now. For the first time since she had started school, Lisa and Jenny were becoming friends. Before, they had fought most of the time over petty things like who got into the bathroom first, or whose turn it was to set the table, but not anymore. Now Jenny got the family together to play games, or urged Lisa to watch old black and white re-runs and made popcorn for them. She would really miss Jenny.

Lisa sighed and shifted position in the backseat. Her parents were quiet in the front. They, too, seemed to be lost in their own thoughts.

They were off the freeway now in a part of the city where many of the older homes on large lots had been passed over in the rush to the suburbs and the rede-velopment of center city.

Mrs. Carson directed her husband up a main road and located Maple Street.

They turned the wrong way the first time, but a second try brought them up in front of an old Victorian house set back from the street in a yard overgrown with trees and shrubs. A sign outside announced "The Haven."

"Come on, ladies. Let's check the place out," Mr. Carson said when he had parked. Neither Lisa nor her mother were in any hurry to get out.

An eager-faced girl in an advanced stage of pregnancy opened to their knock. Her face fell when she saw them and her eyes seemed to grow dull. She admitted them to an impressively paneled room, obviously once a reception hall, now apparently a living room. The TV was on and another very pregnant girl was watching a young woman, who had apparently just won something on a quiz show, screaming on the screen.

"We're looking for Mrs. Lester," Lisa's dad said.

"I'll get her," the girl mumbled.

But she didn't have to. A tall, pleasant-faced young woman was coming through the glass doors that led to the office space.

"You must be the Carsons. Won't you come into my office?" she said cordially.

The room behind the glass door had been divided into several smaller offices. She ushered them into the one marked "Social Worker," and when they were settled, asked, "How much do you know about our facilities?"

"Nothing, except that you take care of unmarried

pregnant girls," Mr. Carson answered.

"We feel we have as fine a facility here as anyone in the country," Mrs. Lester said.

You'll have to prove it to me, Lisa thought, but then had to admit that no "facility" would be appealing to her.

"We have complete prenatal care for the girls. There is a nurse on duty twenty-four hours a day, and a doctor comes from St. Luke's Hospital to hold a clinic here once a month."

"They go to the hospital from here?" her mom asked.

"Yes. The three senior OB residents take turns coming here so that the girls will know the one who delivers their baby." Mrs. Lester looked closely at Lisa, then asked, "When are you due?"

Lisa glanced at her mother, but she let her answer for herself. "Early November."

"Then you would probably want to come in late August. Most girls spend their last three months here, but some come sooner. We do everything we can to protect the privacy of our girls." Mrs. Lester frowned and glanced toward the waiting room. "Those girls shouldn't be out there, but they're waiting for company today. Several of the girls went home this weekend, but these girls haven't been here long enough. You have to be here at least a month before you are permitted an overnight at home. You need that much time to adjust to our program."

It sounds like a prison, Lisa thought.

"I'm sure you'll have lots of questions, but let me

show you our facilities and perhaps we can answer them as we go." Mrs. Lester got up and led them toward the door.

Back in the dark entry hall, two pairs of eyes followed Lisa as Mrs. Lester led them up the wide oak staircase. They made Lisa think of the eyes of the frightened baby rabbit Patches brought in once. Lisa felt a sense of relief as they turned at the landing and were shielded from those haunting eyes. Would she look like that too if she came here?

Upstairs the social worker showed them a bedroom. Lisa had only the vaguest impression of a room with three beds that made her think of a monk cell, but lacked even that privacy. She'd have to look at two more girls growing heavy and awkward while the same thing happened to her.

"We have room for twelve girls. There are two three-bed rooms and three two-bed rooms. Just now we have two empty beds, but it varies," Mrs. Lester commented as they went on down the hall, and she opened another door.

"This is the library and study room, but there are no classes today. We pretty much follow the school calendar. Each girl brings her own books, because each school is different and they are in different classes. We have three teachers who come in to help them individually. The girls usually do very well. This is called our Opportunity School, and homework and tests are sent back to the home school. It's understood that the girls are here in a tutorial program. Most who come here have been having trouble with their schoolwork, so schools are glad to go along with the plan."

"So, basically the girls are in a private school?" Mr. Carson said. "I'd almost decided that's what Lisa needed anyway."

That was news to Lisa. Was her dad really thinking of sending her away to school?

Next they saw the small infirmary, and continued on down the hall into the annex where Mrs. Lester paused before another closed door. "We have something here that few homes have, a nursery for the babies. Every girl brings her baby back here from the hospital."

At the word *nursery* Lisa gasped and stepped back. A nursery. Real live babies. Was she ready for this? Did it matter? It was like hide-and-seek, "Here I come, ready or not."

"You don't have to go in if you don't want to, ever," Mrs. Lester hastened to add, seeing Lisa's expression.

"I'd love to—" her mom started, then she too caught Lisa's mood and finished, "No, we don't need to go in now."

"Why do you have a nursery?" Mr. Carson asked.

"The girls come back here for a week after delivery, and we bring the babies here too. It gives the girls a little more time to make the final decision. Some hold and feed the babies; others have nothing to do with them. But both babies and girls need the medical observation that we can give to be sure everything is all right."

"Do they see the baby if they are giving him up for

adoption?'' Mrs. Carson asked. ''Isn't that new? I always thought they didn't see the baby if they weren't keeping it.''

Lisa's thoughts wandered. *A baby. The end of all this. My baby.* It was still incomprehensible to her. *Something swimming around inside me now is going to be a real-live, flesh-and-blood baby, or already is, and that's why I have to come here.* She knew it, but somehow the reality was slow to dawn. She couldn't explain to herself why she didn't want to see the nursery. Was she afraid to confront reality?

''Giving up a child is almost the same as having it die,'' Mrs. Lester was explaining as Lisa began to listen again; ''and if the girl sees it, she has a better focus for her grief. Grief is a normal part of the healing process.''

''But how many can give up a baby after they see it, Mrs. Lester?'' Mrs. Carson persisted.

Mrs. Lester smiled, ''Please call me Donna,'' she said before she continued her explanation. ''Many do decide to keep the baby—for a while. That's another advantage of the nursery. Immediately after childbirth is a highly emotional time, and we try to discourage them from making a decision too quickly. We urge them to go back home and put the baby in a foster home until they see how they feel once they are back in their own world. Actually, about 80 percent of the girls who come here do give up their babies.''

Back in my own world? Can I ever go back to my own world? Lisa wondered. *Give up my baby? Can I?* She realized that the pain of that decision would be with her for many months, perhaps forever.

"Most give them up?" Her mom was incredulous.

"They get counseling and emotional support here that they wouldn't get under most circumstances. That helps them," Donna said.

Her dad nodded. "I can see that."

Lisa's mom was very quiet for the rest of the tour through the cheerfully decorated sun room, where three more girls with the same haunting eyes were watching TV, and on down the back steps to the clean, well-lighted kitchen.

Here Donna introduced them to the nutritionist and cook, and explained, "The girls get carefully planned meals, and they take turns setting up, serving tables, and cleaning up."

Like home, my real world, Lisa thought. *We have to eat. We have to do dishes. We have to try to study. Home. I'll miss it.* Lisa was homesick already.

They were moving through the dining room with its three round tables, where they ate family style, and on to a room with a Gothic ceiling and stained-glass windows.

"This is our chapel. We're very proud of it. We hold nondenominational services here after breakfast on Sunday morning, and the girls are expected to attend unless they have made arrangements to go somewhere else," Donna said.

Mr. Carson was the only one who commented.

Lisa was thinking about their church at home, not wood paneled, no stained glass there. *I'll miss it, too,* she thought, but then Jesus' words flashed into her mind, "I am with you always." *Yes, Lord, I suppose you are here too,* she acknowledged silently.

"We have a game room and a room for arts and crafts in the basement. Would you like to see them?" Donna asked as they left the chapel.

Mr. Carson said "Yes," and Mrs. Carson said "No," both at the same time. Then everyone looked at Lisa, who hadn't said a word through the whole tour.

"You cast the deciding vote," Donna laughed.

"If I'm going to live here, I might as well see it all," Lisa answered with a stiff smile, hoping she had struck a light note.

At last Donna led them back to her office and gave them each a booklet that spelled out what was expected and what to expect.

Lisa leafed through it quickly. She spotted "Holidays: special meals, snacks, parties, and other activities are provided during these times in order that residents can look forward to holidays away from home." Lisa almost felt like laughing. Look forward to holidays away from home? How could you look forward to that? It wouldn't be Christmas without the family. Then she realized with a sense of relief that she wouldn't miss Christmas and probably not Thanksgiving either.

She flipped on: exercise program, fire drill, phone, smoking, mail, even stamps and change. *They thought of everything, except how I get through three months here,* Lisa thought. *No one can answer that for me.*

"I think we've pretty well covered everything," Mr. Carson said.

"Do you want to make a deposit on a room while you're here? Sometimes we can't take a girl when she wants to come if she isn't signed up ahead," the social worker said.

"It sounds like a good idea," he said.

"Is it refundable if we change our mind?" Mrs. Carson asked.

"We would refund it if the decision didn't prevent us from filling the space," Donna replied. "Our business manager's office is next door. I can give her the check for you. Here's the application." She pulled a form from the desk and handed it to Mr. Carson.

"I'll see the business manager," she said.

At last Lisa found herself back in the car. She ran her hands over the plush seat and thought of the sofa in the living room at home where she wanted to be, to stay. The car dodged through city traffic and onto the freeway toward home.

When they were well on their way, her mother finally spoke, "Dave, we can't leave her there."

"Why not? It looks like a good arrangement to me."

"But it's so institutional."

"Not that bad. Sounds like they take an interest in the girls and their problems. How about it, Lisa?" Her dad raised up and peered at her in his rearview mirror.

I don't want to go, she thought. Then she thought about her mom's nursing course. "What about you, Mom? Are you going to go back to nursing this winter?"

"No, I've decided not to. I'll stay home with you," she announced.

How like Mom, Lisa thought. *She's always giving*

up things for us. Dad wanted to go to Florida in the winter, but Mom would never consent to leaving them, even if Grandma Carson would stay with them. Mom was always buying material to make new clothes for them, but it was rare for her to make something new for herself. Lisa remembered Jenny saying that it was her mom's turn now.

"Can't I stay home and Mom still go to nursing?" Lisa suggested.

"I don't want you home alone," Mom declared. "It would be too boring. Too little to do. Too lonely."

Lisa was hearing her mother describe her own position. *Her turn. Mom's turn. She gave up nursing because she loved Dad more. She'd give it up again because she loves me.* Tears sprang to Lisa's eyes. *It's not fair. I can't let her do it. If I love her I owe her something too. It's not her fault I got myself into such a mess. It's not fair to ruin her plans because of what I did.*

"Mom. I want to go to the home," Lisa announced as firmly as she could.

Her mother, who had turned around to look at her, studied her face carefully. "You don't have to, you know. I probably won't go back to nursing this year anyway. I would really enjoy having you at home."

Kind of like before I started school, Lisa thought, *when she let me bake tiny pies of leftover crust and tear up lettuce for the salad. No way. I don't need that now. I've got to grow up.*

"I like the idea of keeping up with my class. I think it would be easier with a group than if I tried to do it alone," Lisa insisted. As she talked she realized that she was trying to convince herself as well as her parents.

"Are you sure?" her mom quizzed.

"I'm sure. They have good facilities, and I'll be better off there under the circumstances." Lisa was beginning to believe it.

"Good girl," her dad said.

11

A bell was ringing insistently. It called Lisa from a deep sleep from which she didn't really want to awaken. Gradually she realized why. This wasn't her own comfy double bed; she was cramped on a much narrower bed. *Where am I? Oh, it's The Haven,* she realized. She was alone, on this unbearably hot afternoon in August, in a double room that was all beige—walls, wooden floor, and drapes—nothing like her own room with its big mauve roses on the wallpaper, white ruffled curtains, and the plush mauve carpet she could wriggle her toes in.

Her parents had left her here this afternoon after her dad had carried her things up and her mom had made her bed and put her pink elephant on it. She had stood on the wide veranda and watched their car drive away. She continued to stand staring at the spot where she had last seen them until her eyes watered. Mrs. Davis, the nurse on duty, had finally come out on the porch, put her arm around Lisa, and led her into the house.

"Donna has taken some of the girls to the park, but some are upstairs, probably watching TV in the sun

room. Why don't I take you up to meet them?" she had
said.

"I want to fix up my room," Lisa had excused herself. She hadn't wanted to meet anyone until necessary.
She had trudged upstairs alone, thrown herself on the
bed, and escaped into sleep.

A bell rang again, harsh and shrill in Lisa's ear. She
glanced at the small alarm clock her mom had plugged
in on the chest so she could see it from the bed: 5:20.
That must be a warning bell for supper. The nurse had
told her supper was at 5:30. She didn't care.

The room, shaded by a tall tree outside the window, was already in deep shadows. Lisa rolled over and
faced the blank wall. It reflected her feelings perfectly.
Life was a blank, a great big three-month blank to be
endured until she was free again. If only she could sleep
until it was over.

She closed her eyes and envisioned her mother at
the stove in their country-style kitchen with its oak cab-
inets and the windows draped in blue and white chintz
facing the sunny yard. How she wished she were there
helping her set the table, or even peeling potatoes, a job
she hated. How often she had complained about being
called away from a predinner TV show. If only her
mother were calling her now, she'd be quick to help.

There was a firm knock on the door, and a busi-
nesslike voice called, "Lisa, time for dinner."

Lisa didn't move even when she heard the door
open and someone enter. She closed her eyes until she
felt a hand on her shoulder.

"Come, dear, you've got to eat dinner. No one is

allowed to miss a meal unless she's really sick," the voice said.

It compelled Lisa to obey—*like a prison guard,* she thought. Lisa rolled over and opened her eyes to see a woman with graying hair in a white uniform.

She introduced herself as Mrs. Wallace, the afternoon-evening nurse. "From suppertime on I'm the only staff member here except Mr. Purdy, our maintenance man, who lives here. Part of my job is to see that you get the proper nutrition. Come on now. Get up and comb your hair. Everyone will be waiting for us."

Lisa did as she was told and soon found herself crowded at a table with six other girls to whom the nurse introduced her before they sat down. One table was empty, and a man with thinning gray hair and a wrinkled face, Mrs. Wallace, and two other women in white were sitting at the staff table.

Dishes piled with steaming food were ready to pass, and Adele, a black girl sitting next to Lisa, began handing them to her as soon as Mrs. Wallace finished asking a blessing. Lisa automatically filled her plate, but only picked at the food. Nothing looked or tasted good to her. She compared it to the meals at home in their own cheerful dining room. The plain white dishes and vinyl-covered table were such a drab contrast to the colorful placemats her mom always used under their flowered pottery dishes.

She looked around this table at the six strange faces and was ready to run back to her room when an older girl across the table addressed her.

"Where are you from, Lisa? By the way, I'm Holly. I know you didn't get many names just now, but it won't take long to get acquainted."

Then came more questions from the others about her age, family, and school. Lisa was being drawn into the group almost against her will. Holly began to fill Lisa in on the rest of the girls.

"Cassie has a sister too, don't you?"

Cassie, who like Lisa had been picking at her food, seemed to see Lisa for the first time. "Yes, she's fifteen. Oh, that's how old you are, isn't it?" Cassie seemed to brighten.

"Cassie's only been here a couple of days," Holly, who looked as if she wouldn't be there much longer, volunteered information about Cassie again.

Conversation soon became general, and at last supper was over and the girls drifted into the reception hall. Holly explained that they usually went upstairs, but when it was so hot it was cooler to stay downstairs. Besides, they would have to come back for exercises.

Nothing but news was on TV, and the girls seemed to be ignoring it, but Lisa was used to watching news. Her parents and Jenny would be sitting in the den now watching Dan Rather expound on the events of the day. The open windows would be letting in a good breeze and Patches would jump up in her lap. Suddenly she missed Patches most of all.

Lisa couldn't concentrate on the news. She wanted to curl up on her bed again, but when she started for the stairs, Holly called, "How about joining us for games in the sun room after exercises?"

Lisa shook her head, "No. I've got to get my things organized in my room." She used the same excuse as before.

Back in her cell, she threw herself on the narrow bed and wished it were a single room. An empty bed made it even lonelier.

She drifted off to sleep again until awakened by a knock. Holly stuck her head in the door and called, "Exercise time."

"I'm too tired," Lisa mumbled.

"No excuses accepted," Holly said. "It's part of the game plan. Everyone exercises."

Having agreed to live by the house rules, Lisa dragged herself up and started downstairs with Holly.

On the way down Holly asked, "When are you due?"

Lisa glanced at Holly's extended stomach and awkward walk, and a great feeling of relief swept over her. Here she could talk about her pregnancy. She no longer had to watch every word for fear she would let something slip.

Her folks had discussed whether or not telling people she was going into a tutoring program was dishonest. Her dad had finally settled it by pointing out that Joseph was going to put Mary away privately when he found she was pregnant before the angel told him that she was carrying the Son of God. If it was right for Joseph, it was right for them to spare Lisa from being branded with a Scarlet Letter. Her father's tortured face rose before her as they turned on the landing and descended to the entry hall.

The rest of the girls were lined up on the carpeted floor. The exercises Mrs. Wallace led them through were simple enough for Lisa, but it was evident that for Holly they were becoming difficult. As the girls squatted and tried to rise to a standing position with their hands still on the floor, some of their abdomens almost touched the floor too. Several of the girls, led by Adele, got to laughing, and before she knew it Lisa was laughing too. They laughed their way through the "pelvic rock," an exercise designed to strengthen the abdominal muscles and make carrying the baby easier. It was funny to see the other six girls on the floor with bent legs pushing their abdomens into the air.

Mrs. Wallace didn't discourage the laughter, and Lisa was almost sorry when exercise time was over. Little did she think she could ever laugh at herself in this situation.

She realized that she had never answered Holly's question about her due date. When they were dismissed, she went directly to Holly and with a sense of freedom told her. She then asked when Holly was due.

"Any time. I was one-finger dilated when the doctor last examined me," Holly said casually. "Come on up and play a game with Cassie and me. There's nothing but reruns on TV."

Lisa surprised herself by agreeing. She had determined that she was going back to bed as soon as she was free. Cassie was the one who was reluctant to join in, but Holly was insistent. "Anybody else for UNO?" Holly made a general invitation, and Adele offered to play too.

Holly led the way up the steps. Halfway up the first flight, she paused with her hand on her stomach.

"You okay?" Adele asked.

"This critter is sure acting funny tonight," Holly replied.

"Maybe you had better get Mrs. Wallace to check you," Adele suggested.

"No, I'm okay," Holly insisted and went on up the stairs. As they shuffled and dealt the cards, Holly shifted again and again in her chair.

"You sure you're not in labor?" Adele asked again, and even Cassie looked at her closely.

Lisa was getting worried. Was Holly really ready to have her baby? Lisa's stomach churned as if she were riding a roller coaster. "We'd better get the nurse," Lisa urged.

"Not yet," Holly seemed so calm. No one was interested in cards now except Holly.

"Aren't you afraid?" Lisa was surprised by Holly's composure.

Holly laid her hand on her stomach again and smiled at Lisa, "What's there to be afraid of? We're well prepared for childbirth. They've taught us what's going to happen." Then a shadow passed over her features, and she said wistfully, "Only once he comes, he's not mine any longer."

"You're giving him up?" Adele sounded disbelieving. "I didn't know that."

"But that's why I came here." Holly sounded so sure of herself and so reasonable. "I'm going to finish college. It wouldn't be fair to him to keep him when I can't get a job to support him."

"I'm keeping mine," Adele was emphatic. "You can get Aid to Dependent Children. That's what I'm going to do no matter what Mom says. I'm not going back to school. I hate it."

Cassie, as well as Lisa, was listening closely.

"Did you meet with the adoption agency counselor?" Holly asked.

"I don't want to meet with her," Adele declared. "Besides, who would want to adopt a black baby?"

"It might be a good idea to see what she has to say," Holly said just as she reached for her stomach again and grimaced. "I guess I'd better see the nurse."

"Want me to get her?" Lisa asked.

"No. I'll go down to the infirmary," Holly said, getting up to go. She stopped a minute, looked at Cassie and suggested, "If I go to the hospital, Cassie, why don't you move in with Lisa. I'll be back here only a few days after he's born."

Cassie glanced shyly at Lisa. Lisa smiled, "Would you? I'd like that. The room seems so lonely with an empty bed." She turned again to Holly. "You'd better get down to the nurse."

Cassie moved into Lisa's room to sleep after they had seen Holly off to the hospital. The next morning when Lisa and Cassie came downstairs, the other girls were crowded around the bulletin board. There beside the sign "No Smoking, Fetal Growth in Progress" was a typed bulletin: Holly Clark had a 6 lb., 12 oz. baby at 5:10 A.M. Mother and baby doing well.

"What was it? Boy or girl? Why doesn't it say?" Lisa asked Adele.

"If you don't keep your baby, you might not want to know what sex it is," said Tina, the tall, slender girl who sat across the table at dinner. "If we don't know, we can't tell her."

Lisa was startled. She hadn't considered not knowing what sex her baby would be, but suddenly she understood. If you know, everytime you see a baby of that age and sex you would wonder if it were yours. But that would be foolish. You couldn't keep on thinking that way. But if you didn't know the sex, the baby would never be real, much like her feelings now. It was still hard to visualize that what was happening inside her was no longer "it," but instead a real baby.

She wandered in for breakfast still deep in thought, so much so that she was only vaguely aware that she wasn't the only one not talking. Each girl seemed as much lost in her own thoughts as Lisa. She didn't taste the egg, but she must have eaten it, for her dish was smeared with yolk when she left the table. *I've got to know what sex my baby is,* she argued with herself. *I can't carry him all this time and not know.*

It had been tacitly agreed when she came here that she would give the baby up. Now she was wondering, *can I?* She knew she would soon have to meet with the adoption counselor. Was she ready to decide? What was the right thing to do? How could she know how she would feel when it was all over, next year, the year after, on and on? Could she ever forget this child she was carrying? He would be born of her body. Nourished, given life by her. *Mine. He's mine!*

Mrs. Davis was standing at her place at the staff table ringing a little bell. Lisa finally glanced up at her.

"Girls," she announced, "Mrs. Lester is planning a shopping trip for you this morning to a new mall. It's just opened and I think you'll find lots of exciting stores to explore. It's not required, but I encourage you all to go. It should be enjoyable."

Lisa thought of the Saturdays she spent at the mall with Debbie and then this summer with her mom and Jenny. She looked around at the girls at the table.

Adele spoke first, "Hey, man, that sounds great!" Cassie was still pushing egg around on her plate with a vacant look on her face and Holly was gone. Lisa missed her even though she had known her only one evening. Lisa knew what she must do, "Hey, Cassie, doesn't that sound like fun?"

Cassie glanced up at Lisa, and a faint smile tugged at the corner of her drooping mouth, "I guess so."

Fun, it wasn't. At every turn there was another baby being wheeled by in a stroller, asleep, laughing, crying, or gurgling. Never had Lisa seen so many babies in one place, or was she just more aware of them? And Holly? And herself?

Lisa began studying mothers as they passed. Some looked happy, others didn't. She saw a young mother take a swat at a pretty little girl, and another grab a little boy and drag him along at a pace too fast for his short legs. What made the difference? She looked at Adele and wondered what kind of mother she could make at seventeen. *And me? Would I be a good mother?* She pushed the question aside.

They had come to Gordon's department store with its high fashions.

"Hey, Cassie." Lisa took her by the arm and steered her over to the window. "How do you like that?"

The other girls followed to gawk at the mannequin in a ridiculous outfit that none of them would ever wear.

"That's just what we need with our maternity tops. It'd give us balance at the bottom," Adele commented. Even Cassie had to laugh.

12

$\mathcal{D}$onna stopped Lisa on her way into the building after their shopping trip. "The lady from the adoption agency will be here this afternoon. I've scheduled you to meet with her at 3:30."

Lisa's stomach did a flip as if she'd just crested the top of a wave and was tumbling down the other side, "I . . . I don't know what I want to do."

"You don't have to make a decision now. Most of the girls meet with the adoption agency counselor to find out what the situation is. She won't pressure you," Donna explained.

On schedule that afternoon, Lisa found herself in the small office next to Donna's, confronting Teresa Gezira, the adoption counselor.

Teresa began by assuring Lisa that she was there to help, and then opened the way for Lisa to ask questions or talk about anything that was bothering her.

"How's it going at the home here?" Teresa asked with a warm smile. "How do you feel about the other girls?"

Lisa lowered her eyes to the new ring on her finger, a gift from her mother before she left home. It was a small cameo set in silver that Grandma and Granddad had given her mother when she was sixteen. It had been promised to her when she reached sixteen, but her mother had told her she wanted her to have it now. Lisa wore it on her left ring finger, and now she twisted it with her other hand. Slowly she began to share her feelings about Holly not seeing her baby. She wondered how Holly could do it.

"Think about it for a little," Teresa said. "I think I hear you saying that you'd want to see your baby, to know its sex. Lots of girls do. But why do you think Holly didn't?"

"I suppose it would be harder to give it up if you knew whether it was a boy or a girl," Lisa voiced her thoughts.

"Do you think it would make any difference in your decision?" Teresa encouraged her to explore her own feelings.

"I can't tell yet," Lisa answered. "But I'll want to see him, to hold him after all the months of waiting." She pushed the cameo between her fingers and straightened it again.

"What will your next step be after you know?" Teresa led her to think further.

"I suppose I might want to keep it," Lisa confessed.

"What would that involve? How do your parents feel about it?" Teresa asked.

Lisa pushed her ring around with her thumb before she acknowledged as she had before that it would be almost impossible. She admitted as much to Teresa.

"Does it seem that the reasonable and fair thing to

do would be to put the baby up for adoption?" Teresa asked sympathetically.

Lisa nodded, and Teresa turned the conversation into more general lines. Before she let Lisa go, she asked her to think more about adoption and bring any questions she might have when she saw her in two weeks.

Cassie was carrying the rest of her things into Lisa's room when Lisa returned from her counseling session. Donna had encouraged the move, saying, "Holly would probably like to be alone when she comes back. It might make the transition back to college easier for her."

Cassie dumped an armful of clothes on her bed, and Lisa helped her hang them in the closet. Lisa didn't feel very talkative, but she was concerned for Cassie, who hadn't said a word. To draw her out, Lisa commented on her attractive maternity tops, asking, "Where did you get them?"

"My mom made them," Cassie said, but offered nothing more.

"Does she sew much for you?" Lisa was determined to make conversation.

"Not usually," Cassie answered.

"You mean she's just been sewing since you got pregnant?" Lisa was surprised.

Cassie only nodded.

"My mom sews for me all the time, but she doesn't do much fancy work." Lisa thought of the Easter dress, the last thing she had made for her. Lisa could still get into it, except it hitched up now at the waist. But her mother hadn't sewn for her since she was pregnant. She had just bought three inexpensive tops, a skirt, and a pair of hot pants, and told her they would do. Cassie's things were lovely.

"My mom didn't make any maternity clothes for me," Lisa said.

"I guess Mom's trying to buy me off with these," Cassie said abruptly.

"What do you mean?" Lisa was puzzled.

"Kevin and I wanted to get married, but she wouldn't let us." Cassie's voice was bitter.

Cassie's only fourteen, Lisa thought, and caught herself before she blurted out that she agreed with Cassie's mother. Instead, she asked, "How old is Kevin?"

"Eighteen. He graduated from high school in June, and he's learning to be a computer repairman. We could have managed," Cassie replied.

"Brandon didn't want to marry me." Lisa was glad she could say it without bitterness. Poor Cassie. *How sad to be angry with your mother,* Lisa thought.

"We're going to get married anyhow, as soon as I'm old enough," Cassie said, suddenly coming to life. "I'm going to put the baby in a foster home until we can support her. It's our baby. They can't make us give it up. My sister, Karen, is the only one who understands. Dad sides with Mom, but then it doesn't matter 'cause he's got a new wife and I don't think he really cares what any of us do. Mom wants me to finish school. She says Kevin may say he loves me now, but what about ten years from now? Who cares about ten years from now? I know he loves me and will take care of us."

Lisa understood how Cassie would want to keep her baby, but even while doubts were flooding Lisa's mind about giving up her own baby, Cassie's ideas seemed shaky. She suspected Cassie wanted Kevin to take over for her dad. Cassie was so young. Fifteen suddenly seemed so much older than fourteen.

Lisa shared her own story with Cassie, adding, "I was dumb to think Brandon loved me. But at least, with God's help, I've forgiven him. Before I came here I sent him a note telling him so, and asking his forgiveness for the nasty remarks I was making about him in school, but I never heard from him. . . ." Her voice faltered. "You're lucky if Kevin wants to marry you. You are sure about Kevin?"

Cassie said firmly, too firmly, "Yes, I'm sure of Kevin."

After that conversation, Cassie and Lisa became good friends, talking openly with each other. Both were concerned for Holly when she returned. She was much quieter than before and excused herself from activities, saying she was too busy getting her clothes ready for college.

Lisa was relieved to see how slim Holly looked and hoped she would be the same way after her baby was born. She felt so terribly fat now.

One morning Lisa saw Holly pause at the nursery door. The baby was just behind it. Holly put her hand on the knob and then jerked it away and hurried on down the hall. A few days later Holly was gone, though the baby was still there waiting for the adoption process to be completed.

It was time now for Lisa's next meeting with Teresa, and Lisa had some questions.

"Is there any way I could give up my child long enough to finish school and then get him back?" she wanted to know.

"Yes, you could put him in a foster home for several years, or I should say homes, because it could mean that he would be moved several times. How would you feel about that?" Teresa said.

"What are foster homes like?" Lisa asked.

"The child-placing agency picks the foster home as carefully as possible. Most foster parents are fine people, especially those who take babies. They usually love them very much. But often people who love young babies don't want the care of a toddler, and that's when it becomes necessary to move the child. How long would it be before you'd be able to care for your child?"

Lisa considered. Two more years of high school, plus two or three years to get an R.N. "Four or five years."

I'll miss so much of his growing up, she thought, and asked, "Would I be able to see him?"

"Yes, you have the right to visit, usually Saturday afternoons," Teresa replied.

"I could hold him only for a little while and then those other people would get to be with him all the time," Lisa expressed resentfully.

"What would they be expected to do in order to take care of him?" Teresa wanted Lisa to think about it.

"Hold him and feed him . . . and change his diapers, and fix bottles, and get up at night." Lisa tried to remember some of the things her cousin talked about. "It's a lot of work, I guess."

Lisa's mind raced on, "You say the foster parents don't mind, but would the baby mind being moved around? Would he even know when he is so young?"

"What do you think?" Teresa turned the question back to her.

"I asked you." Lisa resisted thinking too hard about it.

Teresa answered this time, "Psychologists think they do. They believe first impressions are very important."

"He'd know if he was moved?"

"Babies become attached to the person who takes care of them. They call it bonding and it happens early," Teresa told her. "When they lose the person who takes care of them, how do you think they might feel?"

Lisa remembered how she felt the day her parents left her here at the Haven. She was fifteen and understood. How could a baby who couldn't understand deal with it? A phrase from a favorite hymn of thanksgiving ran through Lisa's mind, "For the love which from our birth over and around us lies." That love had been there for her, though she had betrayed it. What chance would her baby have without it? Yes, her parents had always been there, and she wouldn't be able to "be there" for her child.

"Who would adopt my baby? Do I have any say in

the kind of people who would get him?" she wondered aloud.

"We try to match your baby with a family as similar to yours as possible," Teresa replied. "We have so many more applicants than babies that we have a long list from which to choose."

"These are couples who have never had any children?"

"In most cases yes, though some already have a child of their own and for one reason or another can't have any more, or some already have an adopted child and want another."

"I think that would be nice, to be adopted into a home that already has one adopted child. You'd have someone in the same situation as you."

"What kind of situation do you visualize that as being?" Teresa probed.

A discarded person, one that your own parents didn't want, popped into her mind, but she didn't say it. Almost immediately she thought of a family in the church with two adopted daughters. They didn't look like discarded children. Both were beautifully dressed, popular girls with happy smiles. She supposed that their parents loved them as much as her parents loved her and Jenny; and while everyone knew they were adopted, she couldn't really detect any difference in the way the church people treated them. As she thought of it, she wondered if in some ways people treated them better than they treated Jenny and her. Why would that be? Did they feel sorry for them underneath? Anyway, they seemed happy enough.

"It's a good situation," Lisa finally answered, then plunged on to the next question. "Could I know who the family would be who gets my baby?"

"Not by name, but you'd know all the pertinent facts about them. You can be sure of one thing, that they are emotionally mature. That's the main thing, along with compatible backgrounds in religion, education, and economic status. We study the family in their home and have a feel for these things."

"You mean they'd go to the same church I do?" Lisa chose the most important point to pursue.

"Not necessarily the same denomination, but we'd try to find a family with the same kind of religious convictions that you have," Teresa assured her.

"I'd like that. It's very important to me now." Lisa explained to the counselor what Jesus Christ meant to her.

Teresa listened sympathetically. "I understand," she said. "There are many families who feel the same way. If you're interested, next time we meet I can give you a profile of a family I think you could approve."

Lisa's stomach felt like she was on a roller coaster again when she went for the next session with Teresa. Would she have to make her decision today? Teresa was nice, but Lisa knew the time was soon coming when she would have to give a final answer.

Teresa filled her in on a family who had already adopted a boy, now three years old, who wanted another child to complete their family. The father owned a business like Lisa's dad, and was doing well. They were active in a church similar to Lisa's. In fact, the

wife's parents were missionaries who were ready to re-
tire and live close by, so the children would have the
advantage of an extended family relationship. The first
child was doing well in the family, and Teresa had every
reason to expect the situation would be good for Lisa's
baby.

This sounded like a good family, one Lisa could
trust to raise her baby as she would want him to be. She
twisted her ring round and round on her finger as she
considered the details of what Teresa had told her. Just
then the baby began to move and suddenly gave an extra hard kick. Was he agreeing? Or was he objecting to
being given away by his mother?

*You can't be impulsive when you give a baby away.
You can't get him back if you change your mind,* she told
herself. *It's so final. Like I died—or he died.* There was
still a moving in her stomach. Was his little fist demanding a place in her world?

Lisa put both hands to her head and rubbed her
temples. It felt as if two fists were inside jabbing into
either side of her head. "I don't know yet what I want
to do," she said.

"That's okay," Teresa assured her. "You have six
weeks or so to make up your mind, and lots of girls
don't make a final decision until after the baby is born.
But remember it takes a while to process an adoption,
and the younger your baby is when he's placed the better for all concerned. Let's talk some more about your
plans for the future."

Teresa led Lisa to talk about her goal of becoming

a nurse, and then asked, "Do you think you'll ever want to marry?"

Lisa stared at the tile floor and twirled the ring on her finger. It was on the finger where she would wear a wedding band, if anyone ever wanted to give her one. Married? Deep inside she'd always hoped that someday someone . . . She had twisted the ring off and it slipped to the floor and rolled away. Teresa retrieved it in mute respect for the difficulty Lisa now had reaching the floor.

When she put it back on, Lisa finally answered, "Yes, but I was never attractive to boys before. Lots of girls in my class had boyfriends when they were way back in grade school, but I never did. I didn't think boys liked me until Brandon . . . and he didn't really like me either. Who would ever want me now?"

"Lisa, you're more beautiful than you know. Brandon found you attractive because you *are* attractive. Others will be drawn to you, too, when you let them know the real you."

"Do you really think so?" Lisa didn't know whether to believe her or not.

"Of course. But my point is, how do you think having a baby, if you keep him, would affect your prospects for marriage?"

Lisa had a ready answer for that question, "If he were the right kind of person, he'd love my baby too."

"But how about you? Would you want to start marriage with a ready-made family? How might the baby feel about having to share his mother when he'd had all the attention up till then? These are things you need to think about."

That night sleep didn't come for Lisa as easily as it usually did. Her mind replayed the questions and possibilities that Teresa had raised. Just now it was hard to believe anyone would ever want to marry her—but what if someone did? She remembered how she and Jenny used to vie for attention from their parents, especially their dad, and there wouldn't be any dad to give extra attention . . . unless Dad . . . No, she rejected that possibility.

She had only the faintest recollection of a time before Jenny was born, of Daddy kissing Mommy while Lisa clamored to be picked up. It was always Daddy who picked her up at that point. Could she expect that of a man who married her? Could he respond to her child like her own father did? The child might be six or seven, not two or three. She thought about seven-year-olds. Some weren't that cute anyway. That was expecting an awful lot of any man to take on a child that old, or even a little child. No, it wouldn't be fair to him. How would she have felt as a child if Mommy were her whole life and suddenly she had to share her? She had resented Jenny, and that was a normal situation. *The situation for me and my baby won't be normal. No, it won't be fair to the baby to expect him to share me with a stranger, but if I don't marry, will it be fair to try to raise my baby without a father? That's not fair either.*

Not fair, not fair, not fair—the words hummed in her brain—*go to sleep—not fair—go to sleep—not fair.* Nothing was fair. She must be fair to her parents, to her baby, to a possible husband, to herself. How? Turning on her side and moving an extra pillow under her distended stomach as the nurse had shown them, she beat on the pillow with her fist.

What should I do?

"Pray again," a voice inside prompted. She had been praying and reading her Bible every night, but she still didn't know what to do.

She heard Cassie's even breathing. She was asleep, and Lisa didn't want to disturb her. Lisa pushed the extra pillow to the bare wooden floor and quietly eased her heavy body onto her knees.

"Lord, you know what's best for my child. Please help me make the right decision," she prayed softly.

She rested her head on her arms and tried to recall the sermon the chaplain had for them at the worship service last Sunday. It had been about guidance. He said God had a plan for every life if we let Him show us. How was it? Read the Bible, pray, and consider the circumstances—that was it. He said God leads us in the paths of righteousness. She remembered because she knew she had left the path of righteousness and was so thankful for Christ's forgiving and accepting love.

But what's right for the baby? Does the Bible speak of adoption? Lisa wondered if it would disturb Cassie if she turned on the bedside light. It might. She pushed herself to her feet and by the light of her alarm clock located her Bible and waddled out of the room.

The sun room was empty, though one light burned through the night. She chose the chair beside it and lowered herself into it.

She was so glad the Bible Grandma Carson had given her last Christmas had a concordance where important words were listed, telling where they could be found. *Adoption, here it is.* Some verses in Romans 8: "waiting for adoption," "received the spirit of adoption," and in Galatians, "God sent his son to free us from bondage that we might receive the adoption of sons." It seemed as if the Bible compared coming into Christ to being adopted. God gives us all the privileges of sons and heirs. Certainly the Bible recommends adoption into God's family. Ultimately that's the only adoption that counts.

Lisa prayed again over her open Bible, "Lord, please, no matter what, adopt my child into your family."

The minister had said some other things, too, about guidance—that we had to be willing to think, to look honestly at the future and at our own motives.

"I've tried, Lord. I've tried." Lisa knew what she must do. It was as clear as adding up an arithmetic problem.

———

When Lisa met with Teresa Gezira two weeks later, she told her to go ahead with the adoption process. Lisa was still scheduled to meet with Teresa every other week until the baby was born, but for Lisa things were settled, or so she believed.

After her session with Teresa, Lisa checked their mailbox. She had the usual note from someone at home, and today there was a letter for Cassie too. In the past six weeks Cassie received very few letters from anyone and no visits from Kevin. She and Lisa had both had their visit home at the end of the first month, but Cassie had had little to say about it when she returned.

Lisa glanced at the return address as she carried the letter to the room. It was from Karen, not Kevin.

Lisa was disappointed.

Cassie tore it open eagerly and began to read while Lisa settled herself on her bed to read her own letter. Suddenly Cassie threw the letter on the floor, stamping on it and screaming at the same time, "She's lying! She's lying!" Then she threw herself on her bed, sobbing so hard that Lisa could see the bed vibrate.

But for her weight in front, Lisa would have leaped up. As it was, she reached Cassie as fast as she could and tried to comfort her, patting her gently on the back. As Cassie quieted, Lisa asked, "What is it?"

At last Cassie struggled to a sitting position and answered, "Karen says she saw Kevin at the drive-in movie with another girl. I don't believe it. Mom put her up to writing that."

"At night she might have been mistaken," Lisa tried to reassure her, but Lisa didn't really believe that. Cassie had expected Kevin every weekend. He hadn't come, and she never heard from him except when she telephoned him. "Why don't you ask him about it the next time you call?" Lisa suggested.

Cassie's face was blotchy, but it was the look in her eyes that worried Lisa more. It reminded her of the look she had seen in the eyes of a neighbor's dog that had been hit by a car. She rescued it and could still feel its heart pounding against her palm. She wondered if Cassie's heart was pounding too.

"I'm afraid," Cassie said in a small voice.

Lisa wrapped her arms around her as best she could. "Don't be afraid. If it's true, better to know it now than marry him and have him run around on you. This might sound corny, but maybe it's for the best. Cassie, I believe God loves you. God is our Father in heaven who cares about us and works even bad things out for our good eventually. I really believe that, Cassie, and all this could be part of His plan."

Cassie shook her head slowly, "I don't know. We never went to church much, but I used to go to Sunday school when I was little. We sang 'Jesus Loves Me.' You know, I really believed that then, but not now."

"Well, you can, because He does love you," Lisa said. She knew it would take time for Cassie to get over Kevin's unfaithfulness, but she prayed silently that Cassie would come to see that her mother was right after all and not go on blaming her.

"If Mom would just have let us get married, this wouldn't have happened," Cassie said, but she didn't sound convinced. Lisa thought again of Brandon. At least he was honest from the time he learned she was pregnant.

Lisa went on to share with Cassie her decision about the baby and could see Cassie listening carefully to all her reasons. Two weeks later after discussing it with Lisa, Cassie, too, told her counselor to look for an adoptive family for her baby.

13

As Lisa fell into the routine of The Haven, the weeks passed less slowly, and at last her due date was near. School had begun shortly after her arrival, and she was doing well with her studies this year. Each week there was a clinic where they received a thorough examination and lectures to prepare them for childbirth.

The last month Lisa decided not to go home. She was afraid someone might see her and the purpose of coming to The Haven would be lost. Her mother had discovered a private school that took girls any month of the year, and Lisa had agreed to go there until the January term began at her high school. It, too, had a tutorial program similar to The Haven. Lisa wasn't anxious for another change, but she didn't want to fall behind in her studies. Her mom had decided to enroll in the nursing program and had such glowing reports that Lisa was determined to graduate with her class and begin her own nursing course.

It was early November. The tree outside Lisa and Cassie's window had flamed in October and burned itself out. That afternoon its bare branches let in the faded November sunshine. Now bright moonlight traced delicate shadows of the branches on the wall above Lisa's bed as she woke up feeling wet. She lay still, concentrating on her stomach. It seemed as if the baby was on his hands and knees, pushing his back against her abdominal wall. Come to think of it, it had felt that way for several days. Now she realized this must be the contractions the instructor had tried to describe in class. Lisa felt no panic; she had been well prepared. *I'd better tell the nurse,* she thought, lumbering out of bed and stopping to catch her breath as her stomach balled up again.

She glanced at the clock. *Should I time the contractions?* she wondered, and decided it would be best to follow directions and tell the nurse how she felt. By moonlight she found her slippers and padded quietly to the door. Before she reached it, Cassie stirred and said, "Lisa, is that you? You okay?"

Lisa answered, "I think I'm ready to go to the hospital. I'm going to see Mrs. Wallace."

Cassie struggled out of bed and switched on the light, "You lie down. I'll get her."

Another cramp grasped Lisa's abdomen. She was glad to let Cassie go, and eased herself onto the edge of the bed, preferring to wait sitting up than to cope with lying down and getting up again. *I hope this is it,* she thought. *It'll soon be over.* Yet with the thought came a pang. In the last month especially she had become more and more aware of the baby as a person. The resident had shown her where his head, back, arms and legs were located. His vigorous kicking amused her, especially when the doctor tried to listen to his heart. Often at night before she fell asleep, she felt a special closeness to him. When he was born it would indeed be over, and a great sadness filled her.

She was distracted by another contraction and stifled the impulse to fight by tightening her abdominal muscles. *Relax.* That was the word for early labor. *Think happy thoughts,* the nurse had suggested. *It will help you to stay relaxed.* Happy thoughts! How ridiculous. What happy thoughts could she think? *Mom, Dad, and Jenny love me. Jesus loves me. God loves me.* She said this over and over to herself.

Soon Mrs. Wallace was in the room with Cassie. "Lie down, dear, and let's see how things are progressing," she said.

Lisa eased herself back down on the bed, wincing with another harder contraction. Mrs. Wallace placed one hand on Lisa's extended abdomen and checked her watch. Lisa concentrated on keeping her arms and legs loose and, breathing slowly, whispered to herself, "Mom loves me."

Mrs. Wallace nodded. "That was a good contraction. I think we'd better get you to the hospital. You have everything packed you'll need. You don't have to dress. I'll get the car, and you can meet me at the side door."

Mrs. Wallace checked under the bed for the suitcase and picked it up. "Why don't you just wrap up in a blanket," she suggested as she left.

The time was really here. Lisa began to shiver. Was she cold, or was it part of labor? She was on her feet, going to the closet for her coat. What did they tell us to do if we shivered? Take a deep breath and hold it.

Maybe I will try the blanket, she thought. But Cassie was ahead of her. She had already stripped the blanket from Lisa's bed and was wrapping it around her shoulders.

"I'll go down with you," Cassie said. Ungainly as it was for Cassie, she kept her arm around Lisa as they waddled down the steps.

The car lights gleamed in the cold November night as Mrs. Wallace swung under the portico.

"This is it, I hope." Lisa tried to smile, but another contraction caught her just then and she stopped, waiting for it to pass before she went out to the car.

"God bless." Cassie gave her a squeeze before she let her go.

Lisa clambered in beside Mrs. Wallace, pulled the blanket around her, and closed her eyes. She was still shivering. She'd try holding her breath.

"The car is cold. It'll take a few minutes to warm up," Mrs. Wallace said.

Lisa let out her breath, but now her teeth were chattering. Yes, the car was cold. At least the hospital wasn't very far.

"You realize, Lisa, that I can't stay with you. Once you're admitted, the hospital will call one of the woman volunteers to come and coach you if you want them to. You did want to deliver without anesthesia, didn't you?"

"Yes," Lisa answered weakly. Another contraction hit and she remembered to breathe into her chest deeply, or was that shallow breathing that was supposed to relieve pressure on the uterus? She couldn't remember.

The city streets were quiet; even on the boulevard traffic wasn't heavy.

"Remember, you don't have to go all the way through this without relief. You can ask for help any time you feel the need, and they'll give it to you. Heroics aren't necessary," Mrs. Wallace said as they stopped for a traffic light.

"But I want to be in control," Lisa said. Control was the word their birth instructors had all stressed.

"And so you should be. They won't use anything that will put you out of your head. Just something to help you relax, or relieve the pain if you need it."

Soon they swung into the hospital driveway marked Emergency Entrance. When they pulled up to the door, Mrs. Wallace got out. "Wait here," she said. "They'll bring a wheelchair for you, and I'll be right back."

A wheelchair sounded like a good idea to Lisa as another contraction hit. She filled her lungs again with a long deep breath and let it all out slowly. A young man in white swung the door open, helped her into the wheelchair, and pushed her into the brightly lighted waiting room. She closed her eyes against the glare. She wasn't sure how long she sat there, but she had another contraction before Mrs. Wallace came back with a handful of papers.

"They'll take you up to the labor room now. These papers are for the nurse up there," Mrs. Wallace said, giving them to the orderly. "Good luck, dear. I have to get back now, but the hospital has called your coach. It's Mrs. Blum. I think she taught some of your classes. She'll be coming soon to help you through labor."

Lisa remembered her as being as pretty as she was knowledgeable. She was always so interested in helping the girls with their breathing exercises. *I hope she gets here soon. I can't remember anything for sure about how I should breathe,* she thought as a pain came again. *Relax.* It was hard to do in a wheelchair.

At last they were on their way. She was pushed down the hall to the elevator, whisked to the fourth floor, taken into a cubicle divided off from a larger room by a white curtain, and settled into a high bed with side rails. Someone on the other side of the curtain was moaning.

I want Mom, the thought rose. It was impossible. Why had she ever decided to come here, so far away from Mom and Dad? Lisa was still shivering. She tried holding her breath again, and the shivering slowly subsided.

When would Mrs. Blum get here? *Relax.* It was easier now that she was lying down, except for the nurse fussing around. She had a hospital gown for Lisa, which meant sitting up, pulling her own gown off, and slipping into the sack that was open in the back and barely covered her thighs.

"That's better," the nurse said. "Now we can prep you."

The nurse took Lisa's blood pressure, listened with a stethoscope for the baby's heartbeat, and checked to see how much she was dilated.

"Everything's fine. Would you like some medication?" the nurse asked.

"No," Lisa said, "I want to be in control."

"Good girl." The nurse patted her leg. "Dr. Chang is on duty tonight. He'll be in to see you later," she said as she slipped behind the curtain to attend the girl next to Lisa, who had just cried out.

Lisa felt sorry for the girl. She sounded so frightened and out of control. *I won't be that way,* Lisa assured herself, *because I've been taught what to expect.*

Another pain hit. *Relax.* Lisa took deep breaths until she felt dizzy. Then she tried holding her breath, and her head cleared. *If only I can sleep,* she thought, but the light was too bright. She closed her eyes anyway. More crying came from behind the curtain. *Control. I must keep control.*

How long she lay there trying not to fight the more frequent contractions, she didn't know, but she opened her eyes as someone gently lifted her hand. It was Mrs. Blum.

"You're awake," she said with a smile. Her shoulder-length black hair was pulled back tonight. "The nurse tells me you're doing fine and are well into active labor."

"How should I be breathing?" Lisa asked.

"It's time to breathe high in your chest, just shallow breaths like we practiced. That way you'll keep your diaphragm off your uterus."

A contraction came again and Lisa tried changing her breathing. It seemed to help.

"Would you like me to massage your abdomen?" Mrs. Blum asked.

Lisa agreed readily. Mrs. Blum leaned over, placing both hands with her fingertips at the bottom of Lisa's enlarged stomach and firmly, but gently, rubbed up and outward over the distended area. She kept it up as long as the contraction lasted while Lisa took short, shallow breaths as the nurse directed.

When the contraction passed, Lisa smiled faintly at her and said, "Thanks." It was good to have her here. Maybe it was just as well that her mother wasn't. She'd probably get upset.

"Are you relaxing between times?" Mrs. Blum asked.

"I'm trying," Lisa answered.

Mrs. Blum lifted Lisa's nearest arm and ran her hands down from shoulder, to elbow, to wrist, to hand. "You're relaxing very well indeed, Lisa," she said. "I don't think you need help to relax your arms and legs, but we'll work on the uterus."

Soon another hard contraction hit, and Mrs. Blum's strong hands were there. When it was over, in the interval before the next one, Mrs. Blum got Lisa into a semi-sitting position, "That's better," she said, "gravity will help."

"My back aches," Lisa panted.

Mrs. Blum helped her turn on her side, then rubbed Lisa's back. It gave some relief, but the pains kept coming with a greater frequency and more intensity. Time stretched on, punctuated by the nurse's visits until early-morning light colored the window. Pushing aside the divided curtain, Dr. Chang came into the cubicle and examined her.

"It won't be long now. You're just about fully dilated. Would you like an epidural so you won't feel any more contractions?" he asked. "We can put an anesthetic around the nerves coming out of the spine."

Puffing away in the midst of another contraction, Lisa was unable to answer, but she knew she didn't want any needles put in her spine. She shook her head.

Mrs. Blum answered for her. "We'll let you know if she does. I think she wants to stay in control and do it all herself."

Lisa was now gasping involuntarily, for the pains seemed to come without letup.

"I think we better take her to the delivery room," Dr. Chang decided.

An orderly came to help the nurse wheel Lisa's bed into a white sterile room where they transferred her onto a table similar to the one in her doctor's office at home and placed her feet in stirrups. Mrs. Blum, who had accompanied her, explained that it would make it easier for the doctor to deliver the baby. The delivery-room nurse was about to strap Lisa's arms to the sides of the table when, much to Lisa's relief, Mrs. Blum intervened.

"That won't be necessary," she said. "Lisa doesn't plan to have any anesthetic. She'll be alert the whole time."

Through the blur of almost constant pain, Lisa had the impression that the large light at the end of the table was a giant's eye beaming at her.

Dr. Chang hurried into the room and examined her again.

"You're doing great," he said. "We can see the top of the baby's head now.

"Time to start pushing," Mrs. Blum instructed, but Lisa didn't need to be told. She had a great inner urge to push as the pains came now in continuous waves like storm-driven breakers pounding the shore. There was no letup.

No time to think—hold on—control—push—control. Lisa wanted to curl in on herself just like the baby was curled up inside her.

"Do you want anesthetic?" someone asked.

"How long?" she gasped.

"Not much longer now. Look at me. We'll breathe together." It was Mrs. Blum. "Breathe. Push."

"I . . . think . . . I can," Lisa whispered to herself.

"Look at me. Open your eyes. Together now, watch me," Mrs. Blum ordered. "We breathe in . . . breathe out . . . push."

Lisa was vaguely aware that Mrs. Blum was working almost as hard as she was. Lisa worked in unison with her. "I think . . . breathe in . . . I can . . . breathe out," her mind worked as if hypnotized.

"Episiotomy now. Just a little shot first to numb the area," someone warned.

Lisa scarcely noticed the cut they made to prevent tearing the birth canal through which the baby would pass. Something jabbed her too, but it wasn't until later she discovered in her arm an intravenous needle attached by tubing to a bottle hanging from a portable pole. Lisa was now almost in a trance, but she was still in control. At last she distinguished Dr. Chang's order, "Okay. Bear down once more. That should do it. His head's right there."

"Look in the mirror," Mrs. Blum directed. "You can see him coming."

Lisa fought her way back to reality long enough to take a quick look. She saw a round fuzzy ball between her legs. She felt like laughing, or was it crying? No time now.

"Once more," Dr. Chang said.

With all the strength Lisa had left in her weary body, she pushed.

"That's it!" the doctor exclaimed. "His head is out. Just rest a minute while we suction out his mouth and nose."

Lisa heard a cry. She was amazed he was able to cry before he was entirely free of the uterus. She could still feel his feet wriggling up under her heart as if he were glad to stretch out at last.

"Do you want to know what your baby is?" Mrs. Blum asked gently.

"Oh yes, I want to know!" Lisa gasped.

"We just have to get the shoulder out and the body will follow easily," Dr. Chang told her.

The next contraction wasn't as hard as the last one, and she watched in the mirror as Dr. Chang pulled the baby from her, but she couldn't see whether it was a boy or girl.

"You have a little girl," Dr. Chang announced, laying the baby on Lisa's abdomen. She lifted her head to examine the baby. She was covered with a white greasy-looking substance.

"Is she all right?" Lisa asked.

"Fine," everyone said at once.

Lisa could see for herself that all the tiny fingers and toes were perfect. "What's all over her?" she asked.

"Just a natural lubricant," Dr. Chang assured her.

"We'll wash and weigh her and you can hold her in a few minutes," the nurse said.

Lisa watched in the mirror while Dr. Chang clamped and cut the cord, thick as her thumb, that was attached to the baby.

Lisa felt another contraction. She had thought it was over.

"Is it twins?" she said weakly when it passed.

Everybody laughed, and Dr. Chang explained, "No, it's the placenta or afterbirth." In her excitement and relief Lisa had forgotten about it.

The baby was on the outside of her now, pressing in, instead of on the inside kicking out. Her weight on Lisa's stomach felt good. Lisa was studying her baby's hands again when the nurse picked her up and carried her away. Lisa had a terrible feeling of emptiness. She was tired. So tired.

14

*L*isa was still tired when she went back to The Haven two days later, but the girls crowding around to see the baby gave her a lift. Right now the baby was still hers, and the girls were so excited that she couldn't help but be pleased too.

"She's beautiful," Cassie cooed.

"For a 'whitie.' " Adele was kidding, and everyone laughed. "You're lucky to have it over with. You came in after we did, and you get to leave first."

"But I waited longer to come. Besides, you're both due any day," Lisa felt the need to answer.

Mrs. Wallace met them as they came up the steps and took Lisa and the baby to the nursery. It was the first time Lisa had entered the room with its row of plastic bassinets just like the ones in the hospital. It looked so sterile. She didn't want to leave the baby there. *I want to hold on to her,* she thought. Just then the infant wrinkled up her still-squashed face, opened her tiny mouth and, with fists waving, began to cry. It was the first time she had cried when Lisa held her, and all her efforts to quiet the baby were of no avail. It was with a rush of relief that Lisa turned her over to Mrs. Wallace.

"Why don't you take a rest now until dinner. You can feed her at six if you'd like."

Lisa was glad to comply with the suggestion. She had an overwhelming desire to escape into sleep as she had on her first day there. But Cassie, full of questions about the delivery, followed her back to their room. Lisa sensed Cassie was frightened in spite of all the classes, and did her best to assure her that it was the way they said it would be.

"You really went all the way through without anything?" Cassie marveled.

"Yes, but you don't have to. Remember, it isn't some kind of contest. If you want something, don't feel guilty about asking for it. I think I would have if she hadn't come when she did," Lisa said.

Then Cassie asked the question that was uppermost in Lisa's own mind. "Are you still going to give her up, now that you've seen her?"

Lisa lowered herself onto the bed as slowly as if she were still weighted down with the baby inside and rolled over to face the wall.

"I don't know." Lisa's tone was somber.

Recognizing her need to be alone, Cassie said, "I'll let you rest now. See you at supper," and left, closing the door quietly.

At supper Lisa was still the center of attention as the girls repeated many of the same questions Cassie had asked about the delivery. Cassie and Adele were the only ones left of the group who had been at the table the first night. One by one the others had delivered and gone home. Lisa was ready to go home even if she couldn't stay there long now. She didn't belong here anymore, except . . . except for that room upstairs and what it held of herself.

She was glad when dinner was over and she could go back upstairs to feed Rachel. *Rachel,* the name rose quietly. She knew she shouldn't choose a name for her, but there it was. Rachel, so much loved by Jacob that he worked fourteen years for her. Am I willing to work fourteen years for my Rachel? The question hung unanswered in her mind as she pushed open the nursery door.

Mrs. Wallace brought out a bottle, though Lisa's breasts ached with milk she dare not give, and settled Lisa and Rachel in a comfortable chair. Lisa cradled the baby in her arms and watched, totally fascinated as she had been from the first day, as her baby's miniature mouth worked so hard to pull the formula through the nipple. At Lisa's touch, Rachel's tiny hand, a copy of Lisa's own, clutched her finger.

Lisa felt as if the little fist had closed around her heart. *Rachel, Rachel, how can I give you up?* Lisa's heart cried silently as the baby drained her bottle.

When it was empty, Mrs. Wallace took the infant and sent Lisa away. "We'll take care of the night feedings unless you want to come for the 10 P.M. one."

"I'll come," Lisa said.

Ten o'clock found Lisa back in the nursery and Rachel squalling at the top of her not-so-tiny voice.

"What's wrong?" Lisa asked, feeling as much distress as the baby seemed to be expressing.

"I think she's colicky. See how she draws up her

legs. It's nothing to worry about. Why don't you let me give her some warm sugar water, and you go to bed."

"Are you sure she's all right? Shouldn't we call a doctor?" Lisa worried.

"No, we don't need a doctor," Mrs. Wallace laughed. "It's not unusual for babies to have a fussy period in the evening."

Evening. Mom and Jenny would need to study. *And what about me? I won't be studying at all for a while if I take her home.* Mom and Dad didn't want to see the baby, and they wouldn't let Jenny see her either. Mom had said, "Since you've decided to give her up, I think it would be easier that way." How Lisa wished she could share the baby with them, but it was all settled— or was it? She could still change her mind.

Lisa dragged herself back to her room and got ready for bed before Cassie came in from watching TV. She didn't want to talk any more tonight.

When she lay down, sleep wouldn't come. All the old questions she had wrestled with before writhed through her head. It had always come back to what was fair for everyone, but now that Rachel was here, Lisa found that she was uppermost in her thoughts.

She had been told that if she kept her she could get Aid to Dependent Children, but what would it be like for Rachel to live on welfare? She thought of the welfare families she knew in school. There was still a certain stigma attached to them, and they never seemed to have had much chance to get ahead. No, it wouldn't be fair to Rachel to raise her on welfare when she could be in a home that could give her everything she needed.

Besides, Lisa thought, *I might need more than financial aid.* She remembered the young mother in the mall striking her child for no apparent reason and recognized how bewildered she felt when Rachel cried. Could she cope alone? At sixteen? No. It wouldn't be right to deprive Rachel of the kind of home Lisa had with her own mother and father to care for her. Lisa knew she needed them both and so did Rachel.

She rolled over in bed. "Oh, Lord, I want my baby. How can I give her up?" she whispered.

Wouldn't it have been easier to have had an abortion, to never have her at all, than to give her up now? The thought came briefly.

Lisa knew this was a lie. "Thank you, Lord, for not letting me kill my child before she had a chance to live."

"But what's right? What's right for Rachel?" she prayed again.

From somewhere a voice seemed to answer. Was it in her own head, or was it from outside? Lisa never knew. "Let her go. I'll take care of her."

She buried her face in her pillow and choked out her reply. "All right, Lord Jesus. I give her to you."

Sobs racked her frame as she cried uncontrollably. Then, slowly her own thoughts began to comfort her. *Rachel will live and I won't carry the lifelong secret that I murdered her.* Lisa heard again her dad's remark about the Scarlet Letter. *I won't wear a scarlet A for abortion,* though she knew she would always carry a longing for her child deep in her heart.

There came now a quiet acceptance of her loss. Tomorrow she would ask the nurse if she could be alone with Rachel for a little while.

As it turned out, the nurse was called away while Lisa was giving Rachel her midmorning feeding. When Rachel finished her bottle, Lisa lifted her to her shoulder, patting her gently as they had shown her in the hospital. Rachel made intimate baby noises in her ear, sounds Lisa knew were just for her, sounds she would always remember. But now Lisa had something she had to say to Rachel. She lifted her from her shoulder and, cuddling her in her arms, bent her face close to her baby. Choking back sobs, she whispered, "Rachel, do you know how much I love you? Deep in your heart always remember that your mother loves you so much"—the words choked in her throat—"and that is why she gave you up."

Lisa thought about the Old Testament story of Hannah, who gave up her son Samuel for the Lord's work, and her words turned into prayer: "Dear Lord Jesus, I give Rachel to you. Take care of her, please. Take care of her family. Make it a good family, a better family because of her. God, help them to love her as much as I do. God, help me." The tears were streaming down Lisa's cheeks and falling on the baby's tiny face. Lisa felt sure Rachel was listening and understood.

"Remember, I love you. I'll pray for you always. I'll never forget you," Lisa promised. "Someday we'll be together in heaven where we won't ever have to part."

Lisa carried the baby to the bassinet, kissed her,

and laid her down carefully. "Goodbye," she whispered. "God bless you."

Lisa turned away just as the nurse returned. "I'm not coming to feed her anymore," she said.

The nurse put her arm around Lisa's shoulder and gave her a quick hug. "It's okay. We understand," she said.

———

Lisa was sitting in study hall gazing out the window at the nut tree whose branches were outlined in snow. It was good to be back in school with all her classmates and friends. Debbie had broken up with Lane and especially welcomed Lisa's return. Going back was made even easier because Brandon had transferred to Monroe. Debbie had heard that he had gone to live with his father. To Lisa, it was almost as if Brandon had never existed.

Appearing before the judge in Donaldstown, Lisa had officially relinquished her daughter. It hurt; no surgery could be worse. Lisa knew she would heal, but the scar, though less noticeable with time, would always be there.

As they had left the courthouse, her mother tried to help. Lisa would never forget her words.

"Honey, I'm so proud of you," she had said, putting her arm around Lisa's shoulder. "Do you know what you've done? You've given your daughter a chance to grow up in a loving home and blessed a couple with the greatest gift anyone could give—the privilege of having a family."

Lisa had smiled weakly, and knew in spite of the pain inside that what her mother said was true. God had helped her make the right decision, and He would heal her in the days ahead.

If you enjoyed this book, look for these other young adult novels by Bethany House Publishers at your local bookstore:

New Girl in Town by Judy Baer
Book one in the exciting CEDAR RIVER DAYDREAMS series. Lexi Leighton discovers that making friends in her new home town is next to impossible—until she gets a date with the most sought-after guy in town. But will she have to compromise her ideals in order to keep him?

Too Many Secrets by Patricia H. Rushford
This first book in the new JENNIE McGRADY MYSTERY SERIES promises intrigue and adventure for young adults. Jennie's summer seems perfect until her grandmother disappears with a million dollars in stolen diamonds. When Jennie enlists Ryan's help in finding Gram, a dangerous search looms ahead.

The Race by Lauraine Snelling
The captivating first book in the GOLDEN FILLY SERIES. Sixteen-year-old Tricia Evanston has loved horses as long as she can remember, and her father has been training her to compete professionally. But when her dad ends up in the hospital, it's up to Trish to win the big race.